A Summer's Lease

MARILYN SACHS

LAUREL-LEAF BOOKS

For Audrey B. Kwit

Published by
Dell Publishing Co., Inc.
1 Dag Hammarskjold Plaza
New York, New York 10017

The author and publisher gratefully acknowledge
permission to quote the lines from:

Fabula de Petro Cuniculo (Peter Rabbit)
by Beatrix Potter on pp. 71–72.
Copyright © Frederick Warne & Company.

"The Blind Girl," from *The Janitor's Boy and Other Poems,*
by Nathalia Crane on pp. 85–86. Copyright © 1924 by
Thomas Seltzer, Inc. Copyright renewed 1952 by Nathalia Crane.
Used by permission of Nathalia Crane (O'Reilly).

Laurel-Leaf Library ® TM 766734, Dell Publishing Co., Inc.

ISBN: 0-440-97787-8

RL: 5.1

Reprinted by arrangement with E. P. Dutton,
a division of Elsevier-Dutton Publishing Co., Inc.

Printed in the United States of Ameirca

First Laurel-Leaf printing—June 1981

Chapter 1

My mother never stopped when I was fifteen. Over and over again she yammered away at me. I kept telling her, "Mama, I'm a genius. I'm going to be a great writer. I don't want to work in an office."

She didn't believe me.

"You want to end up like me? Trying to support three kids on my salary? You think it's fun working in a factory, standing on your feet all day?"

"I'm never going to work in a factory, Mama. I'm going to be a great writer."

"Sure, sure, sure! And who's going to support you? Listen to me, Gloria, take a commercial course, learn bookkeeping. You'll get a nice job in an office with a nice salary, and you'll meet a nice, refined class of people. A smart girl like you won't have any trouble."

"I'm too smart to work in an office," I yelled at her. "I'm going to go to college and be a writer."

"You're going to be a bookkeeper," she yelled back.

"No, I'm not. You're not going to make me. I'm going to be a writer, and then you'll be sorry, but it'll be too late."

Sometimes my mother smacked me, and sometimes she chased me around the apartment, but most of the time she only yelled.

During the day my mother worked in a toy factory, painting smiling faces on dolls, but at night she came home and usually fought with me or Joe. Joe, my oldest brother, wanted to get married before he was drafted, and she didn't want him to. My mother fought with him or she fought with me. She hardly ever fought with Herby, my middle brother, because he was always sick, and she never fought with my father because he was dead.

When she fought with me, it could be anywhere in the house, but when she fought with Joe, it usually started in the kitchen with the door shut. Not that it remained there. Sooner or later it erupted and burst out of the room into the whole house. I was usually left out of the beginnings of her fights with Joe but generally managed to come in for the ends.

Tonight Mama and Joe were locked in the kitchen —their voices low but hissing.

"What now?" I asked Herby.

He was sitting in the living room, listening to the radio. Even in the dim lamplight his skin looked terrible—full of pussy pimples on his forehead and under his nose. My skin wasn't so hot either but at least I covered it with Pan-Cake makeup. Herby and I looked alike. I hated to admit it but we did. We resembled our mother. The three of us were dark, thin, nervous and long-nosed. Only Joe was round and fair and blue-eyed like my father.

Herby's dark curly hair looked greasy, and nervously I reached up to pat my hair. Whenever Herby's hair looked particularly revolting, it always reminded me to wash my own hair. I hated Herby's hair and I hated mine—dark, greasy, kinky hair. I wanted soft, straight, blonde hair that I could wear over one eye the way Veronica Lake did—the way so many beautiful women did.

Well, I wasn't beautiful—my skin was bad, my hair was ugly, I had hairy arms and legs, and no bust. So what! Who cared? I did. But I could get along without being beautiful because I was a genius, and geniuses didn't have to be beautiful.

Herby wasn't a genius, though. He had asthma, and spent most of the spring and fall wheezing. From September through November, and from March through May, the vaporizer went on almost full time. Now it was late in June, so the vaporizer was off but its smell still lingered.

Mama hardly ever fought with Herby. If she

tried, all he had to do was start wheezing, and she'd say quickly, "All right, all right, Herby, never mind. Forget it. I didn't mean it. Go sit near the vaporizer."

Herby was her favorite. He was going full time to City College, studying to be an accountant.

"What's going on in there?" I said, motioning with my head towards the kitchen.

Herby shrugged and leaned a little closer to the radio. The voices from the kitchen amplified. My mother suddenly screamed, ". . . selfish!"

"Is it Bonny again?"

"Shh! I'm trying to listen," Herby said crankily. "Go away!"

"Drop dead!" I told him, and moved towards the kitchen door. By now the voices were just below screaming pitch, so I had no problem hearing.

"I'm sick of waiting," Joe was yelling. "I put it off two times already, and she's sick of waiting. There's no reason to wait."

Joe wanted to get married and my mother wouldn't let him. Right now he was working for The Big Tomato, a large fruit-and-vegetable stand on 168th Street. The owner, Mike Newman, had a daughter named Bonny. She was kind of a drip, wore a lot of makeup and didn't have too much upstairs. But neither did Joe, for that matter. He was going to be drafted in a couple of months and my mother didn't want to lose his allotment.

"Just wait until Gloria graduates," said my

mother. "Two more years—that's all I ask. Then she'll be working, and there'll be money coming in."

"I'm not going to be working," I shrieked. "I'm going to college, just like Herby."

"Get away from that door," my mother yelled.

"No, I won't," I yelled back. "If Herby can go to college, so can I."

"Herby's a sick boy," screamed my mother, "and get away from that door!"

"I'm sick too," I hollered. "I get sore throats all the time. And besides, I'm a lot smarter than Herby. Even in math I'm smarter than Herby. I get 95's in everything, and he never got anything higher than an 85. I'm not going to work when I graduate. I'm going to college and then I'm going to be a writer."

"You're going to work," screamed my mother. "A girl doesn't have to go to college."

I kicked the door, and my mother opened it and reached out for me. I fled into my bedroom with her hot on my heels, and managed to slam the door in her face.

"Gloria, open that door!" she yelled.

"No!"

"Gloria!"

Herby began whining behind her about how in this house he could never manage to hear anything on the radio.

My mother breathed outside the door for a while, and then went off to make supper. Sooner

or later, I was going to have to open the door since
it really wasn't my room—my mother and I shared
it. We slept together in the big bed that she and
my father had slept in when he was alive. My
socks and underwear filled the two lower drawers
of the bureau where his clothes used to be, and
every morning I looked at myself in the mirror
over the dresser where their wedding picture stood.

My father was the one I liked best in my family
and he was dead.

The only thing that belonged to me in the room
was a small desk near the window. It had orig-
inally belonged to my cousin, Eddie, and I inherited it five years ago when he grew up. It had
a middle drawer that locked, and nobody but me
knew where the key was.

I moved over to the dresser, frowned at my face
in the mirror (there was a new crop of pimples
forming on the right side of my chin), and reached
my hand behind the mirror frame. The key lay
hidden there, in a small space between the frame
and the mirror. I fished it out, opened the desk,
and took out my current notebook.

The drawer held all the others, all eleven of
them. I had been keeping a daily log since I was
nine, six years ago. Not daily exactly—some days I
skipped because I was sick or tired or lazy or
bored—but almost daily. Some days I wrote only a
few sentences, other days pages and pages.

The longest entry was written a few months
ago, on March 27, 1943. That was the first time

anybody besides me realized that I was a genius. For years and years I had been writing—stories, poems, fairy tales and confessions. I wrote bits and pieces of anything and everything. I showed them to anyone who would look, presented them to my mother, my brothers, my relatives, my teachers, and to the very few friends who were willing to read them.

"Go out and play," my mother generally said. "Don't sit with your nose in a book all the time."

"I'm busy. I'll read it later," from Joe.

"It's stupid!" from Herby.

"Very nice! You write very nice," said Aunt Sadie.

A, wrote most of my teachers.

But nobody said I was a genius until Mrs. Horne. She didn't exactly say I was a genius, but I knew she knew I was. She just about said so on a story I had knocked off quickly for my English assignment on March 26, 1943.

> C^+—*You are far too good a writer to get away with this kind of work. For a lesser student, I might grade this A^+, but for someone of your talent, shame!*

I wrote seven pages about Mrs. Horne and about my great love for her. She was the best teacher I ever had. I thought so even before she gave me the C^+. She was smart, intelligent, well-read, humorous, and her manners were refined.

Like me, she may not have been beautiful on the outside, but I thought she glowed with an inner beauty, and she thought I was a genius.

Somebody rapped on the door. "Mama says you should come help her make supper," gasped Herby.

"You help her," I shouted.

"She said you!"

"Well, why don't you help once in a while? You never do anything."

"GLORIA!" came a roar from the distant kitchen.

Quickly I opened my book; dated it June 23, 1943; and wrote only one word, *Tomorrow!*, before hurrying off to the kitchen to protest.

Chapter 2

Tomorrow became today. New copies of the school magazine, *Wings* (June '43), were distributed during our English class. I felt the beatings in my ears as I turned the crisp pages and smelled the good new-print smell. On the contents page I lingered self-consciously. Carefully I glanced over towards Maude Green on my right. She had her elbows on *Wings* and was talking over her shoulder to Mike Presser. On my left, Jerry Lieberman was flipping the pages quickly, not looking my way at all. Nobody sat behind me, so hungrily I began searching the contents page for my name.

Frantically I ran my finger down the page until halfway down I found it.

Jubilantly I examined my name. It seemed to stand out above all the others. Gloria Rein—how gracefully the letters arranged themselves. And Shadows—an intriguing title. If I didn't know me, if I was a stranger glancing at the contents, wouldn't I stop at

Wouldn't I eagerly turn to that page immediately? I did, and nearly felt my heart jump out of my throat when I saw the double-page spread and the huge letters for the title. The first six words of the story were in caps.

SHE LAY ON THE LUMPY COUCH in the living room, looking up at the cracks in the ceiling. Through the tightly closed window the sun streamed, dabbing golden streaks on the dusty furniture.

Mm! I wanted to read it all through again, slowly, savoring each golden word. But first, I

turned back to the contents and resumed my
search. On page 34, I noted with irritation a story
called "Blind Date" by Maude Green. Disgusting!
All that drippy girl ever thought about was boys.
Mrs. Horne had asked her to read the story to the
class back in February, and lots of kids laughed.
Incredible! Later, when she told me it had been
accepted for *Wings*, I just raised my eyebrows.
She probably figured I was jealous, but now she'd
know better, once she checked out the contents.

On page 38, there was a story by Jerry Lieberman. Two for Jerry so far—a poem *and* a story. I
didn't like that. I ran my finger down the contents
faster. There were two columns, and I had to work
through three-quarters of the second column before I found it.

The Icicle and the Leaf—a story,
            Gloria Rein 50

Slowly, with stiff, clumsy fingers, I opened the
magazine to page 50. It was so beautiful, I nearly
cried. The margins around the story were decorated with leaves and snowy branches hanging
with glittering icicles.

WINTER had come again and with it the
frost.

That's the way it began. I read it over again.

WINTER had come again and with it the frost.

What an exquisite beginning! I read it again.

WINTER had come again and with it the frost.

Then I noticed. Only the first word was in caps, unlike the first *six* in my other story, "Shadows." I frowned. Was it an insult, a slight? Did it show a preference on somebody's part for "Shadows"? And if it did, whose? Frantically I turned back to page 26 and examined the first sentence of "Shadows."

SHE LAY ON THE LUMPY COUCH in the living room . . .

How splendid that looked! I quickly turned back to page 50.

WINTER had come again and with it the frost.

That looked splendid too.

Perhaps it wasn't an insult after all. Perhaps whoever was responsible for caps decided that *Winter* should be set off from the rest of the words in the sentence. I had never really considered this use of caps before and began flipping through the pages to check it out. I didn't really want anybody else's story to start with more caps than mine, but, on the other hand, maybe too many caps showed a lack of confidence in the author. I turned to Maude Green's story—four words in caps. Now what did that mean?

I flipped quickly from page to page, checking the caps in each story. On page 60, I found "City Poems" by Jerry Lieberman. And even worse, there were more poems by him on page 61, page 62, and page 63. I stopped worrying about caps. Four pages of poems by Jerry, and each page had a small sketch relating to the poem. On page 60, a solitary figure stood under an elevated train. On page 61, a cat worried some trash in a garbage can. On page 62, some pigeons circled a roof against a night sky, and on page 63—the final page in the magazine—a group of girls jumped rope on a city street.

I quickly read one of the shorter poems.

It was not that good. Perhaps the others were worse. I closed the magazine and tried to calm myself. Jerry had one story in the magazine and a group of poems. I had two stories and no poems. How many poems equal one story?

Talent always made me nauseous—not dead talents like Shakespeare and Dickens and Jane Austen. It was the living talents, and most especially the living talents that I knew, like Jerry Lieberman.

My stomach was churning as I tried to convince

myself that I was not jealous of Jerry Lieberman. So what if his poems were better than mine? So what if they were *much* better than mine? Poetry no longer interested me as much as prose. I needed room, and poetry was like a too tight stocking.

My stories—nobody wrote stories like mine. Nobody! Not Jerry, not anybody else! Not Helen Lewis, the current editor-in-chief of *Wings;* not Frank Donahue, the future editor; nobody! I clenched my fists.

Was I afraid of Jerry? Yes! Yes! Yes! Yes! Today Mrs. Horne was going to announce next year's staff of *Wings.* Of course, Frank Donahue would be editor-in-chief. He would be a senior next year, and had served his apprenticeship as assistant editor in his junior year. The assistant editor always became editor-in-chief. And that's what I wanted—to be assistant editor. Next year I would be a junior, and today Mrs. Horne was going to announce my name as assistant editor for next year. I knew she was going to do it inside every wrinkle of my being. I knew it like I knew I was a genius. Next year assistant editor of *Wings,* and in my senior year, editor-in-chief. I was going to be named today.

And Jerry?

Impossible, I told myself, struggling with my pulsing stomach. Jerry's stories were clumsy and sentimental. He didn't have my range and my control. He didn't have my imagination and my commitment. Look at all the things he was into—

student council, debating team, French club. . . .
All I wanted was to be assistant editor of *Wings*.
He could have everything else. I had been count-
ing on it ever since I started high school. Nothing
else mattered.

I would be a perfect assistant editor—single-
minded and hardworking. The quality of my writing spoke for itself. Nobody compared to me.
Frank Donahue, the new editor-in-chief, wasn't
anything special as a writer—good at interviews
and inspirational editorials maybe, but not out-
standing in anything else.

Once I was assistant editor I could handle Frank
Donahue. I would make changes—not only in for-
mat but in content too. I'd eliminate some of the
sappy, soapy stuff like "Blind Date." Jerry was too
soft. He'd be a good poetry editor. Sure! That's
what Mrs. Horne would probably do—make him
poetry editor. Sure! I didn't really have anything
against Jerry. If he became poetry editor, I could
work with him. Why not?

"That's a beautiful story—the most original in
the whole magazine." Jerry was leaning towards
me, smiling. Damn him! My talent wasn't causing
his stomach to do flip-flops.

"Thank you," I said coldly. "Which one do you
mean?"

" 'The Icicle and the Leaf.' I like 'Shadows' too,
but 'The Icicle and the Leaf' is so delicate, so
unusual. It reminds me of Oscar Wilde's fairy
tales. Have you ever read them?"

"No," I lied, and hated myself for lying. Why did I lie anyway? Just because I enjoyed reading Oscar Wilde's fairy tales didn't mean I had plagiarized anything from them. Why didn't I just say, "Yes, I have read them and think they're marvelous"? I didn't have to say no. I didn't have to worry that he was going to think I filched anything from Oscar Wilde. My story wasn't really anything like Oscar Wilde's. So why did I say no? And why did he ask me about Oscar Wilde in the first place?

"Well, I think you'd like them."

I nodded carelessly and then said, in what was supposed to be a kindly voice, "You have quite a few poems in this issue. I haven't read them yet but I'm sure I'll like them."

He blushed, really blushed, and I looked at him with contempt. He was the only boy I knew who blushed. His pale skin turned red, and he began blinking nervously. He was a fair, rather stocky boy with large, pale blue eyes. He looked like a large rabbit then, and my stomach settled.

"Maybe Mrs. Horne will name you as poetry editor," I suggested pleasantly. "You'd be a good poetry editor."

"I'd like that," he agreed. "What about you? Do you want to be short story editor?"

"No," I told him right out. "I want to be assistant editor."

Jerry's face wrinkled up, puzzled. "But what

about Hilda Burns? Don't you think she'll be assistant editor?"

"No," I told him, "she won't. Hilda will be a senior next year. The assistant editor is always a junior."

"Well, I think she deserves it. She was short story editor this year, and she did a good job."

"Very good," I told him patiently, "and Mrs. Horne will probably let her be short story editor again next year. She's good for collecting other people's stories."

Jerry's face turned red again, and he probably was going to say something else when Mrs. Horne asked everybody to sit down.

Now it was going to happen. Now! Now! Maybe all my life I had been waiting for this moment. Mrs. Horne was talking. She was saying how this class, the sophomore honors English class, was always the most exciting class for her to teach. It was, for her, like charting new territory, like discovering new continents. As faculty advisor of *Wings*, it was always to her sophomore class that she looked for future talent. Her eyes rested on me when she said *talent*. That smile of recognition on her lips was for me, not for Jerry Lieberman, not for anyone else, only for me.

Suddenly I clenched my teeth, remembering. Next year, Mrs. Horne would have a new sophomore honors English class—and she would be looking for fresh talent. I hated that class, and even more, I hated the possibility of some other writer bringing forth that same smile of recognition. At that moment I wanted to stop all future writers from being born. I wanted to take all babies who would develop into writers and put them into baskets and float them out to sea. I wanted all those ninth-graders entering my school next fall screened carefully and all the talented ones put to the sword. I wanted only *my* words, *my* stories to remain.

She continued talking, on and on, about how much talent this particular class contained. False! Only me! I was the only one in the class. Why was she looking at Jerry now? Why? Look how his rabbit face turned bright red. Look at me, Mrs. Horne. LOOK AT ME!

And she did. Now, she said, smiling encouragingly, only at me, was the time to select some of the new editorial staff for next year's *Wings*. Of course, she said, a number of the present staff would remain. Frank Donahue would become the new editor-in-chief, Margaret McCormick would stay on as business editor, Martin Miano would also continue as circulation editor, and Hilda Burns as short story editor.

I smiled at Jerry, but he kept his eyes on Mrs. Horne's face.

She told the class that there would be vacancies on the staff not only for writers but for artists as well, and she started naming some of the people she hoped would join. Hurry! Hurry! Hurry!

The new poetry editor, she said, after careful consideration, would be—I looked over at Jerry, a kindly congratulatory smile on my face—Elsie Brier. Elsie Brier? The new feature editor would be Edward Black; the new management editor, Aron Wilpon; and the new assistant editor— No! I didn't want to hear it. I wanted to put my fingers in my ears and run screaming from the room.

She said this had been the hardest decision since there were two people in the class, two remarkably talented people, either of whom would be a faculty advisor's dream for an assistant editor. Never before, in her sophomore class, had she been forced to decide between two such talented, dedicated students. It was difficult, but now that she had made a decision, she realized that it could only turn out for the best. After all, wouldn't two people of extraordinary ability be twice as good for *Wings* as only one?

Therefore, contrary to her usual practice, she was going to appoint two people as assistant editors, and she proceeded to name them. "Jerry Lieberman and Gloria Rein."

I wanted to throw up. Mrs. Horne was looking at me, smiling at me. Other faces all around the room nodded and smiled. I wanted to throw up. I knocked a book off my desk and bent down to pick it up. If only I could stay down there, under the desk, hidden until I could control the nausea and the fury. Impossible! I leaped to my feet, glanced wildly around the room at all the others behaving as if nothing of importance had just taken place, and fled—hoping I'd make it to the girls' room in time.

Chapter 3

I was washing my face in the bathroom when Elsie Brier came in, looking for me.

"Mrs. Horne wants to see you," she said. "Aren't you excited? I am. I never thought she'd pick me for poetry editor although she did like my poems. She put two of them in *Wings*. But I was sure she'd make Jerry poetry editor—he's tremendous. Weren't you surprised when she made you both assistant editors? I guess I thought you'd get it. Most of us did. But . . . what's the matter, Gloria? Are you sick?"

The more she talked, the sicker I felt. The nausea began rising again, although there didn't seem to be anything left in my stomach. I didn't like Elsie. I never liked Elsie. I didn't like her poems either. I never liked her poems.

"I'm all right," I told her.

"You look kind of green."

"Why don't you leave me alone!" I blazed at her.

"Oh!" She stood there frozen, as if my anger had turned her into a statue. There was still a weak, sympathetic smile on her silly face; so just to get her moving again, I said, "Sure I was surprised. How she ever could have made *you* poetry editor, I'll never figure out."

That helped. She began squirming, and my nausea disappeared. "You really are a louse," she said finally, and slammed out of the room.

I examined my face in the mirror. Elsie was right—it looked green, like an unripe tomato. Now I had to go back and talk to Mrs. Horne. I fished a comb out of my pocket and began working on my hair. I needed to look calm and collected when I talked to her. I needed to appear composed. What was I going to say? I was going to resign, of course. I was going to tell her that I would find it impossible to work with Jerry Lieberman—that we were worlds apart—that there wasn't room for two assistant editors and that I would step down.

What was I *not* going to say? I was not going to say that she had dealt me a cruel and bitter blow by coupling my name with Jerry's, my great talent with his little one. Because of her, I would never again write a story for *Wings*. Her loss would be greater than mine; and in the future, whenever it happened, whenever it became a matter of public knowledge that I was a genius, I would never acknowledge that when I was fifteen, in high school, and hungry for encouragement, I had received any help at all from Mrs. Frances Horne, faculty advisor of *Wings*.

A few kids were standing around her desk, talking, when I came into the room. The bell rang, and most of them took off. I sat down in a seat near the door and waited for the woman who had betrayed me.

I felt numb but calm. After I had stated my position, coolly and with dignity, I would turn from her and slowly, proudly, walk out of the room. And don't slouch, I told myself. I watched her as she rose from her seat and put an arm around Ted Fonaroff's shoulders, laughing at something he just said. Laughing! Yes, laughing. Years later, I would laugh the same way. I straightened in my seat as my mind arranged the details of the interview with the press.

Q. Were there any disapointments in your life, Miss Rein, before you became famous?

A. Only one. It was while I was in high school, and a certain teacher, Mrs. Frances Horne, faculty advisor of *Wings*—she's no longer faculty advisor—she made several

disastrous decisions and the magazine
went quickly downhill. They had to put
someone else in, and, I'm sorry to say, she
began drinking because of it, her husband
left her, and she was eventually fired from
her job. Poor woman, I feel great pity for
her *now*, but . . . (laughter here on my
part) but . . .

"Gloria!"
Mrs. Horne stood over me, smiling. I opened
my mouth to acquaint her with my decision, and
burst instead into loud, wet, humiliating weeping.
"Gloria!"
The same arm that had rested on Ted Fonaroff's
shoulders she now laid on mine. I shook it off.
"Why did you do it?" I cried.
She sat down in the seat next to mine and said
once more, "Gloria!"
"You know I'm better than he is," I sobbed.
"His stories stink. All he can write is poems. He
doesn't know how to do anything else. Why didn't
you make him poetry editor instead of that sap,
Elsie Brier? She doesn't know anything."
"No," said Mrs. Horne, "you're not better than
Jerry Lieberman. Maybe your stories are, but
you're not. He happens to be very talented—his
poems are splendid—but he has another talent,
and that's getting along with people."
My tears were bouncing off the desk now, and

she handed me her handkerchief before going on.

"An assistant editor has to work with other people. It's not enough to write well. You have to be able to encourage other writers, to respect different points of view, and to get along with everybody on the staff."

"I could do all that," I wailed.

"Could you?" she said. "Frankly, Gloria, I don't know."

"I could, I could," I cried.

"You know I admire you very much, Gloria. You're a fine writer and a dedicated one."

I sniffed and waited. Now the conversation was taking a proper turn.

"That story you handed in two weeks ago about the two brothers—I haven't returned it to you yet. . . ."

"Yes, yes?"

Mrs. Horne smiled. "It's a remarkable piece of work for a fifteen-year-old girl. If I didn't know you, I'd almost believe somebody else did it."

"Really?" Now I was smiling.

"Really. And I think we'll put it in the winter edition of *Wings*—our first piece for next year."

"Ah!"

"Of course, as assistant editor you'll have to approve it before we can formally accept it."

I resumed crying. "Why did you do it?" I said again. "You know I wanted to be assistant editor more than anything else. Jerry doesn't care. He would have been happy to be poetry editor. He said so. He's in everything—student council—everything. He doesn't need it. I need it."

"And *Wings* needs an editor-in-chief who can get along with people. Can you do that?"

"If they can get along with me, I can get along with them."

"No, Gloria, no ifs when you're an editor-in-chief. Writing talent isn't enough. That's why I want you and Jerry to share the assistant editorship. I think you'll be a good team. There's more than enough work for the two of you, and . . . we'll see. I'm sure you'll enjoy working with the rest of the staff. They're a particularly nice group of kids this year, and . . . we'll see. . . ."

She seemed embarrassed suddenly, and a new thought dawned. "Do we both have to become coeditors-in-chief?" I asked craftily.

"Not necessarily," she said.

"Could one of us become editor-in-chief?"

"It's possible."

"The one who does the better job?"

Mrs. Horne shook her head. "No bargaining, Gloria," she told me. "Let's just see what next year holds."

Maybe I should have resigned right then and there, but I wanted that editorship. I needed it. For a whole year I had been saving up for it, and to give it up now would leave me bankrupt. The editorship of *Wings* was also proof—not so much for me but for others. See—I'm editor-in-chief of

Wings! See, Mama, see Herby, see Joe, see everybody—I'm the best, that's why I'm editor.

Working with others, Mrs. Horne said. I could do it if I had to. Respecting other writers? Encouraging other writers? What other writers were there? Kids who played with words weren't writers. Kids who wrote a story called "Blind Date" or a poem about brotherhood weren't writers. But I could act respectful and I could pretend to encourage. Their stuff in *Wings* would only bring into proper perspective my own. And Jerry? The nausea rose into my throat and I clenched my teeth down hard. I could handle Jerry too. I could handle anyone if I knew the editorship lay at the end of next year.

"All right," I said, "I'll do it."

"Good girl! Now, there's something else I want to talk to you about. What kind of plans do you have for the summer?"

"Plans?" I wiped my eyes and handed back her handkerchief.

"Yes. Do you have any special vacation plans? Are you going anywhere with your family?"

I looked at her suspiciously but realized that she wasn't trying to insult me. Vacation plans? Some people made vacation plans. She couldn't know that our family never went out of the city together—ever.

"No," I told her. "I don't have any plans."

"Good," she said. "Now let me tell you the kind of plans I have. We usually go to our place in the

Catskills, near Phoenicia. There's my husband and our two boys, Roger and Jason. They were supposed to invite two friends for the summer, but suddenly our plans mushroomed, and now I find I'm going to have seven children all under the age of twelve. What I was hoping was that you might be able to spend the summer with us. You could help me keep the kids happy, and maybe help with some of the chores—everybody will pitch in. But there should be lots of time for you to relax and enjoy yourself. And most of all, you'll be good company for me."

My mind moved quickly—country place, kids, chores, relax, enjoy—it moved through all of that to rest finally on the invitation itself. She liked *me*. She wanted *me* to spend the summer with her. Maybe by the end of the summer she would grow to like me so much she might even reconsider her decision.

"Yes, I'd like to go."

"Good. I was going to ask Jerry to come too. There will be three girls and four boys, so you can divide them up between you. It will also give you both a chance to get to know each other better before all the excitement starts in the fall."

"I've known Jerry since fourth grade," I began angrily, "and I've always . . ." I was about to say "always despised him," but I stopped myself in time. She was watching me, waiting for me to go on, her head cocked to one side, her forehead wrinkled. Why hadn't she told me first that she planned to invite Jerry too? Why did she wait for me to accept before she told me? Would I have accepted if I knew he was coming too? Of course I would have accepted. All the more reason to accept. I couldn't allow him any more advantages than he already enjoyed.

". . . I've always gotten along with him."

"Good!" She nodded approvingly at me. "I think you'll both have a good time—if he can come, that is. I'm so glad you're coming. I never had a daughter, and I'm a little uncertain about how to handle young girls. One of them I think you'll enjoy tremendously. She's very precocious, a tremendous reader, and writes extremely well."

"How old is she?" I asked, hating her already.

"Eleven. Her name is Andrea. Then there's Susie, who's ten, very sweet and friendly, and finally Dorothy, who's only five. I wasn't planning on having such a young child, but her mother, a widow, has a sick father back in Illinois and wants to spend a couple of weeks with him. Are you good with young children?"

"Sure," I lied. I never had anything to do with young children, but I was prepared to do anything to get that editorship. A five-year-old girl couldn't be any harder to handle than a middle-aged woman like Mrs. Horne.

"That's fine. Now, why don't you check with your parents. . . ."

"My mother," I corrected. "My father is dead."

"Oh Gloria, I am sorry." That arm rested on my shoulder again, but this time I let it stay.

"That's all right," I told her. "He died when I was four, and I hardly remember him. But what were you going to say?"

The arm remained there while she talked. She told me I wasn't going to need any fancy clothes— just shorts and slacks and a couple of bathing suits —old, comfortable things. We were going to be out in the country, she said, with no other houses in sight. Maybe we'd get into town a couple of times, so if I wanted to bring along a skirt I could —but nothing fancy. Her hand pressed my shoulder a few times and patted it gently. It felt good.

I nodded as she talked, and even tried to smile from time to time. The pain and nausea were easing, and my mind busily began tidying up and preparing itself for a whole new design.

At home that night I curled up on my bed and opened *Wings* to page 50. My story, decorated with drawings of icicles and leaves, rose up to greet me. How fine it looked! How it healed the sore spots inside me.

THE ICICLE AND THE LEAF
by Gloria Rein

WINTER had come again and with it the frost. All the trees of the forest were bare, and their branches swayed back and forth in harmonic rhythms as they made their obeisance to the new monarch. For Autumn had left in the night.

But before her departure she had woven a beautiful carpet for her successor. It was made from the last leaves of the trees and was of a twisted golden, red and green design. Now the carpet was ripped and torn as the East Wind and the Frost pelted each other with the dead leaves. . . .

I read it over and over again, marveling at its charm and sly humor. It was a romance between the frivolous icicle, daughter of the North Wind, and the vulnerable leaf with his large red heart.

See, see what I can do! I exulted, as I read it, trying to forget how much it sounded like Oscar Wilde's stories. And see, see, turning to page 26, here's my "Shadows," a complete turnabout. Dark and brooding, like a chapter out of Dostoevski, "Shadows" chronicled the agonies in the life of a dying girl. How versatile I was! How extraordinarily talented!

I flipped through the pages, feeling like a queen surveying her domain. But on page 13 I found Jerry Lieberman's poem "The Kite." It was a long one about a beautiful kite of his that had soared too far up in the sky. He had tried to pull it down to earth but the string snapped in his hand and he lost it. Jerry went on and on, comparing his dreams

to that kite. They reached too high like the kite.
They tugged and tugged in his hand, keeping his
mind off the everyday things until, he said, God,
pitying him, snapped the string and took away his
dreams.

What a weak, foolish, clumsy poem, I thought,
and felt the nausea rising again. I stood up and
kicked the leg of the bed a few times until I felt
better.

Nobody was going to take my dreams away.
Not Jerry, not Mrs. Horne, not even God.

Chapter 4

My mother was mad again. Not because I was going away. "Thank God," she said. "You won't be sitting around all summer, moping."

"I never mope," I yelled at her. "I read or I write but I don't mope."

"Did she offer to pay you anything?"

"No."

"Well, I don't know why not. If she had to hire someone to baby-sit those kids and help around the house, she'd pay plenty. Maybe I should talk to her."

"Don't you dare," I screamed. "Just leave me alone. I can handle my own affairs. Don't you dare say one word to her."

"Big mouth!" said my mother, but then she went on to the subject that really angered her.

"Where am I going to get the money for clothes for you?"

"What clothes? I don't need any clothes. She said to bring old clothes."

"Sure, sure! What a rich woman like that means by *old* and what people like us mean by *old* is worlds apart. I'm not having you go up there in rags. I'll borrow something from Aunt Helen."

"I don't want any new clothes," I shouted. "I'd feel stupid wearing new clothes when everybody else is wearing old."

"The way you take care of clothes, they'll look old in no time."

We went shopping at Alexander's, and my mother made me buy two new bathing suits, three pairs of shorts, two pairs of slacks, four shirts and a ruffled, flowered skirt for going out. She also bought me a new pair of sneakers, six new pairs of socks, four pairs of panties and two new pairs of pajamas.

"It's like a trousseau. For God's sake, Mama, I'm not getting married."

"Just shut up, and try on this new bathing cap. I'm not going to have her think you come from a poor family."

"But we are a poor family."

"Well, we don't have to let everybody know, do we?"

My mother grumbled for days and days, but she helped me pack my clothes. And the night

before I was to leave, she came into the kitchen
while I was drinking a glass of water.

"God, it's hot!" she complained. "And the humid-
ity can kill you."

She sank into a kitchen chair and looked up at
me. Her hair pressed damply against her head,
and her face had beads of sweat under her nose.
She was wearing an old, faded slip, and the lacy
inset on the front was frayed. I looked away—
ashamed of her, and happy that I was able to
avert a meeting between her and Mrs. Horne. My
common, vulgar mother couldn't open her mouth
without sounding like the poor, ignorant working
woman that she was. I was ashamed of her, and
ashamed of myself for being ashamed of her.

"Whew!" She picked up a newspaper from the
table and began fanning herself. "Open the window a little more, Gloria."

I opened it, and turned to move out of the room
when she said suddenly, "I do the best I can."

"What?"

"I do my best. It's not easy—three kids with my
income—but I try."

I couldn't believe it but there were tears in her
eyes.

"Uh—Ma—do you want a glass of water?"

She nodded, looking up at me, her dark eyes
shining with tears. They were overflowing one eye
and rolling down her cheek.

"All I do is worry—every day when I wake up, I

start worrying right away and don't stop until I'm sleeping at night."

"Ma!" I didn't want to hear any more. I wasn't used to her like this. I handed her the water, but she put it down and grabbed me, and hugged me fiercely. Since I was standing and she sitting, she had me around the legs and I nearly lost my balance.

"I know how you feel, Gloria, and I wish you had it easier. I wish you could have lots of nice things—piano lessons . . ."

"I don't want piano lessons," I said, struggling to get loose.

". . . and real pretty clothes."

"I don't want pretty clothes. You bought me all that stuff. I didn't even want it. Ma, I have to go finish packing."

She pulled me down into her lap. She had my head jammed against her shoulder, and she murmured into my ear, ". . . and a nice home to bring your friends."

"I don't have any friends." I was struggling to get my head loose, and finally I managed to break out of her headlock. I was sitting in her lap now, and our faces nearly touched. When was the last time we had been so close to each other? I couldn't remember, and I panicked. I broke free, jumped up, and began inching my way towards the door.

She wiped her eyes, blinked a few times, and then said in her normal voice, "Don't leave all those books lying around the room for me to pick up. I've got enough to do."

"Oh Ma, you know I won't. Some of them I'm taking to the country."

"Don't sit around there reading all day long. Get a little fresh air—a little color in your cheeks. . . ."

"I will, I will."

"And Gloria!"

"What?" I was halfway out the door, and impatiently I turned back.

"Have a good time, darling. I want you to have a real good time. Don't worry about anything."

"Thanks, Mama." I hesitated, looking down at her hot, sweaty face, and then I hurried off.

Jerry's brother, Sanford, drove us to the train station the next morning. He was a salesman for a ladies' sweater company, and his samples lay tossed around on the backseat. Jerry had only one suitcase, but I, thanks to my mother, had two.

"That's women for you," Sanford said, grinning at me, as if he knew all about all women.

"A lot of it is books," I told him coldly.

"Sure, honey, I can tell you're a real smart number," he said, heaving my suitcases into the trunk. "But even smart girls will carry twice as much luggage as the sharpest guy."

All the way there, Sanford talked about his job, about women, about clothes, about politics and the army. He had been discharged a few months ago because a Ping-Pong table collapsed on his foot in a canteen. He still walked with a limp but acted as if it was due to some heroic act of bravery in action on his part. He was an authority on everything. He also told silly, coarse jokes—the jerk!

Once or twice I looked over at Jerry, wondering how he could stand having such a boor for a brother. But Jerry seemed to be enjoying himself, laughing at Sanford's jokes, and agreeing with most of his comments.

"Why don't you pick out a sweater for yourself, honey?" Sanford said as we approached the station.

"Thank you," I told him, "but I don't need a sweater."

"Ha!" Sanford said. "Show me the girl who doesn't need a new sweater, and I'll show you a camel without humps."

He laughed knowingly, and I said very slowly, very precisely, "I don't want a sweater."

"Just look over that pile of sweaters near the window. The pink ones with the pearl buttons. Go on, honey, just pick one."

"I don't *want* one."

"You don't have to be shy. Go right ahead. I'm not paying for it."

"I don't . . ."

"You're about a 30, I'd guess, but maybe you'll grow a little. You're still young, and where there's life, there's hope, so you could take a 32."

He forced a sweater on me, which I didn't want and which forced me, painfully, to thank him twice—once for the ride and once for the sweater.

"That's all right, honey, just take good care of my baby brother, here, but not too good care." He gave Jerry a loud kiss on his cheek, patted me on the arm, and finally left us.

"Isn't he something?" Jerry said, looking after him.

"He sure is!" I agreed, almost appreciating my own brothers.

"He's the oldest in the family," Jerry said. "He's twenty-seven, and he's the best-looking."

Heaven help the rest of them, I thought to myself.

"I only hope I'm like him when I'm his age," Jerry said.

I couldn't help it. "Why?" I asked. "Why would you want to be like *him*?"

Jerry's face reddened. "Well, not only because he's so good-looking, but also because he's—well, sometimes I feel so awkward and shy—you've probably noticed—my face gets red when I'm embarrassed and I—damn it—I blush. My brother is so self-confident. I'd like to be like that."

I turned away in disgust and occupied myself with getting on the train. I let Jerry go first, and was able to slip the sweater down the side of the platform before boarding.

"Are you excited about the summer?" he asked after we found seats.

I shrugged and opened my book.

"I am. This is the first time I've ever been away from my family. We've gone away together a few summers—to Rockaway Beach and once to a farm in New Jersey. But I've never been away from all of them for more than a few days. How about you?"

"Neither have I," I told him, "but I'm not worried about that."

"I'm not really worried but I think I'll miss them."

"Not me," I said. "I'm not going to miss mine."

"I'm the youngest," Jerry said, "so I guess I'm lucky."

"I'm the youngest too, but I don't feel lucky."

"Why not? Don't you get more attention than the others?"

"Sure I do. They all pick on me—my mother, my two brothers—I get it from all of them."

"They must be proud of you though," Jerry said earnestly. "You're so talented."

I looked at him suspiciously but his face showed only open admiration. It irritated me and made me uncomfortable at the same time. For me, Jerry's talent was a personal insult. How dare he look at me that way. How dare he admire my work and not suffer pain.

"No," I told him angrily, "they don't admire it at all. Talent is a very disposable item in my family."

He nodded sympathetically. "I guess they don't

take me very seriously at home either, but they act impressed, especially my mother. I suppose most mothers are like that."

"Not mine," I said. "Mine is only interested in money. She couldn't care less whether I write or don't write. She wants me to take up bookkeeping and go to work in an office when I graduate. She's not interested in what I want or what I am." I choked on my words, and knew if I said anything else I'd be crying. So I flipped a few pages of my book, turned away from him and pretended to read.

He let me be. I could hear him fishing around, and finally realized he had a book out too. We both read for a while, and then he asked, "What are you reading?"

I showed him my book, *An American Tragedy* by Theodore Dreiser. "Mm," he said, "I'd like to read that one too. Maybe we can trade books if we both finish our own before the end of the summer."

"What are you reading?"

"*The Magic Mountain* by Thomas Mann."

"I never heard of it."

"Oh, it's good. I've read fifty pages so far. It's a symbolic book. It takes place in a T.B. sanitarium but it's really the world, and all the characters represent different points of view. It's an appropriate book for this summer. Mrs. Horne's place will be our world for the next couple of months, and who knows what the children will be like. Maybe each if them will be symbolic of something strange and mysterious."

"They'll probably just be ordinary, bratty kids," I told him.

I forgot about him for a while as I read my book. Just as my stomach began gurgling, Jerry reached up to the rack above our heads and brought down a large paper bag.

"How about a sandwich?" he offered.

"I brought my own lunch," I told him.

"I told her you would but she insisted on making a couple of sandwiches for you too. Just look at this stuff—she's got enough here for an army."

He unwrapped a sandwich and inspected a Kaiser roll with lettuce sticking out from the middle. He raised the upper end of the sandwich and announced, "Chicken-salad."

I loved chicken-salad but seldom got to eat it. My own mother left the house every morning just as I was getting up and never had a hand in my lunch preparations.

"How about having one at least? My mother will be brokenhearted if she hears you didn't let her feed you."

He held out a sandwich to me. I yearned for that chicken-salad sandwich. My mouth watered for that chicken-salad sandwich. But I couldn't accept anything from him for nothing.

"We could share lunches," I offered.

"Great! What have you got?"

I had my usual—a cold fried-egg sandwich on

white bread. I unwrapped it and divided it in half. The grease had seeped through the bread and it felt cold and clammy, just the way I liked it.

Jerry looked at his half of the fried-egg sandwich thoughtfully.

"You don't have to eat it," I told him proudly. "I happen to like cold fried-egg sandwiches."

He ate it quickly, and then the two of us ate his mother's chicken-salad sandwiches. They were exquisite, storybook sandwiches—just the right amount of tender chicken pieces piled on just the right amount of crispy lettuce, tucked inside a naturally fresh Kaiser roll. She'd also packed hard-boiled eggs, carrot sticks, chocolate cupcakes and perfect ripe peaches.

He had a good life, Jerry did. I watched him eating and chatting, unaware that I was evaluating him. He was soft and spoiled and Appreciated with a capital A. I might eat his food and listen to his talk but I didn't have to Appreciate him or admire him. All I had to do was outmaneuver him, and I could do that.

Chapter 5

July 2, 1943: There are eleven of us right now, but after Sunday there will be only ten. Dr. Horne returns to the city, and will come up on alternate weekends. He will be teaching a course in classical history, and we will be spared his company for most of the summer.

The kids adore him but I find it incredible that an intelligent, well-bred, sensitive woman like Mrs. Horne could ever have married such a man.

Dr. Horne is a classics scholar who teaches at Hunter College. He teaches Latin, Greek, and classical history. I always thought of a classics scholar as someone serious, refined, dark and rather thin. Instead, Dr. Horne is a large, chunky man with a bald head and a loud voice. He isn't refined at all—makes loud, silly jokes, acts like the youngest kid here and is always yelling "Frances" when he can't do something or find something— which is often.

And she caters to him all the time. She never tells him to go blow, which is what I would do if I was stuck with somebody like him.

It seemed strange, at first, seeing Mrs. Horne out of the classroom. Dr. Horne met us at Phoenicia and drove us up to the house. When Mrs. Horne came out of the door in old pants and a faded tee shirt, I felt embarrassed for her. But not anymore. She maintains her dignity wherever she she is and whatever she wears. Even in the presence of her loud, coarse husband, her good breeding only shines the more. All the kids call her Frances, except for Roger and Jason, who call her Mom. They call Dr. Horne Eddie or Dad. I wish I could call her Frances too. She probably wouldn't mind if I did. It seems so silly my calling her Mrs. Horne while the younger kids use her first name.

We had a marvelous dinner tonight. Mrs. Horne is good at so many things. (Only one thing she wasn't so good at, but maybe she will change her mind by the end of the summer.) We had chicken, real baked beans (I never tasted real baked beans before and it was exciting, although I think I like the canned kind better), a huge green salad and brownies. Everybody except Dorothy, who is only five, ate like there was no tomorrow.

If it weren't for the children, I would love it here. Mrs. Horne assumes, since I am a girl, that I will look after the girls while Jerry looks after the boys. I don't know about that. I like the boys better than the girls. Roger, the oldest Horne kid, is eleven, and I think I will like him the best. Jason Horne, who is nine, is cute and friendly, and their two friends, Fred, eleven, and Bobby, nine, seem simple and uncomplicated.

But the girls! Susie—let's take her first because she's the easiest—is Dr. Horne's niece. She is ten, has blonde hair, blue eyes, and smiles a lot. I can't think of any other distinguishing feature but I don't think she'll be a problem. It's the other two I can't stand.

Dorothy is such a baby! Mrs. Horne told me that she'd only be here for two weeks. Her mother is a widow, and needed time to go back to Illinois to see her sick father. As soon as she returns she'll come out and get Dorothy. I don't know how we'll manage that long. Dorothy is a whiner and a crier and a spoiled brat. She hardly ate anything all through dinner, and ended up sitting on Mrs. Horne's lap, sucking her thumb and preventing Mrs. Horne from enjoying her dinner. I know Mrs. Horne expects us to cater to her but it won't be easy. I find children like that repulsive.

Dorothy is bad enough, but Andrea—a stuck-up, self-centered snob, and she's also a Negro. That's not why I can't stand her. I've got nothing against Negroes. Mrs. Horne says her parents

are brilliant. Both of them are docters, the Ph.D.
kind. Mrs. Dr. Fuller teaches at Hunter College
with Dr. Horne. She's an authority on the nine-
teenth-century English poets, and Mr. Dr. Fuller
is the principal of a high school in the city. Mrs.
Horne says that Andrea is an only child, has been
praised too much for her precocity, and needs
some of the rough-and-tumble she can only get
with other children. That's why she's here this
summer.

Mrs. Horne has been telling her parents for
years that Andrea is around adults too much and
needs kids her own age. So she ended up getting
stuck with her for the whole summer. Even
though Roger is the same age as Andrea, Mrs.
Horne thought she should have another girl about
the same age, so that's how Susie was invited.

Anyway, when I first was introduced to Andrea,
she was sitting on the back porch reading. "Here's
Gloria," Mrs. Horne said. "You two should have
a lot in common."

Andrea looked up from her book with that
bored, superior look you sometimes see on the
faces of teachers, as she raised one eyebrow as she
looked me over. If Mrs. Horne hadn't been there
I would have told her off, but I didn't. I said,
"Hi," and then I inquired very pleasantly, "what
are you reading?"

"The poems of Nathalia Crane," she said.

"Oh, I know her," I said. "She was the famous
child poet. I used to love 'The Janitor's Boy.' "

"Yes," she replied, "most people like that one, but they don't know her deeper stuff."

She then nodded at me, and resumed reading as if she were a teacher dismissing a rather backward student.

"Don't be such a show-off," Roger told her. "You're not really reading. I've been watching you, and you never turned that page. You're just acting like you're reading so everybody will be impressed."

Andrea looked at him over her book, just looked at him, up and down and all around as if he were a specimen under a microscope, and not a particularly attractive specimen either. Then she wrinkled up her nose and went back to her book without saying a word.

Roger was sore. They're both the same age, and nobody likes to be put down by somebody the same age. He has a quick temper too, like me, because he went stamping off, banging the porch door behind him. I'm definitely going to like him the best.

After dinner we all went off to play punchball —the kids, Jerry and I, that is—in a field behind the house. All of us went but all didn't stay. Dorothy began crying and quit because Roger told her to stay in the outfield, and she wanted to be on first base. She went back to the house. Later, Bobby fell and banged his knee, and he went off to put some Mercurochrome on it. We played until it grew so dark we could scarcely see one another and our voices seemed to come from far away. It was beautiful.

I loved it, and oh, was I good! I couldn't believe it was me. I've played punchball before, and was always all right, but here tonight, it was different. I was fantastic. I hit the ball harder than I've ever hit it before, and when I ran it was as if I scarcely touched the ground.

Now I'm down in the kitchen all alone. I'm sleeping here like Cinderella. But I don't mind. Every so often, I hear creakings and rattlings, and I'm scared. But I think I'm safe. There are two bunk beds in one corner of the kitchen, and I'm in the top bunk. So nothing can get at me without my hearing it and seeing it first. Except maybe snakes. I wonder if they have snakes up here. I'll ask Mrs. Horne tomorrow. Or maybe I won't.

I never thought the house would be like this—set all by itself in a field, surrounded by mountains. There are no other houses in sight. The house is old, maybe more than a hundred years, and the Hornes have modernized it with an up-to-date bathroom and a big, bright kitchen downstairs where I am. Lucky me! I get to sleep alone because there's no room upstairs. I've never had a place to sleep all by myself, and I think I could get used to it very easily. Dr. and Mrs. Horne have one bedroom, and the three girls have the other. The boys are all together in a sleeping balcony that hangs over one side of the living room. Poor Jerry, he's in with the boys. It's a pleasure feeling sorry for him.

The living room is strange and wonderful. There's almost no furniture in it. Just a long window seat down one side of the room with a huge glass window that looks out over the hills. There's also a great big stone fireplace in the center.

At the back of the house there is a porch that looks like a perfect place for reading, and an old barn that I haven't had a chance to poke into. If only I could be here alone with Mrs. Horne, I guess I'd never want to go back to the city.

Now there is a rustling sound outside the window over the sink. I think I will get down under my covers, bury my head under the pillow, and if it doesn't go away in two seconds, I will run upstairs screaming.

July 3, 1943: I didn't run upstairs screaming. Instead, I fell asleep instantly, and only woke up because the rustling had turned into a loud howling and thumping. It was my first morning in the country, and the children were evidently already up. I quickly washed, dressed and began hurrying upstairs, bumping into Mrs. Horne as she was coming down.

"Well, you look all bright-eyed and bushy-tailed today," she said, smiling and giving me a quick hug. "How did you sleep?"

"Just wonderfully." Loud screams and howls

were tearing the place apart upstairs. "What's going on?"

"It's the children, gently trying to persuade Eddie to rise and shine. Why don't we get breakfast on the table before they remember their stomachs."

Breakfast turned into a disappearing act. I helped Mrs. Horne set the long trestle table and pour eleven cups of pineapple juice. While she was scrambling eggs, I began toasting bread, but before I could finish they all came thundering down the stairs. Then it was all hands and mouths.

Everybody wanted to sit near Dr. Horne. Andrea said she saw ants in the brown sugar, and the others said, "Ick!" Except for Dr. Horne, who yelled, "Where? Where? If there's anything I love, it's ants in my brown sugar." He then proceeded to sprinkle the sugar, ants and all, on his cereal. The kids went crazy—all of them had to sprinkle ants and sugar on their cereal too. Dorothy began crying because there weren't any ants left by the time she got to the sugar bowl. Mrs. Horne just smiled, shook her head, and said, "Eddie! Eddie!" as if she really liked him. Ick!

Mrs. Horne said that all of us would take turns doing the dishes, but that morning, naturally, I got stuck. Mrs. Horne stacked them for me, and then went off to supervise the bed making. Where was Jerry, I wanted to know. His mouth had worked fast enough over the breakfast table, but as soon as there were chores to be done, he disappeared. It was a pattern I was most familiar with. Boys had it good, had it easy—their mothers preferred them to girls, let them go to college, excused them from household chores, and encouraged them to grow up and exploit their wives. Not me! I wasn't going to be part of the pattern, and nobody, not even Mrs. Horne, was going to stick me with most of the housework just because I was a girl.

Savagely I attacked the dishes, managing to break one glass and two bowls before I had finished. I left the sink purposely messy with bits and pieces of egg and soggy cereal. Then I mounted the stairs to the living room, looking for Jerry.

There was only Dorothy, sitting on the window seat below the big window. It was still early in the morning and the mists were rising slowly up on the mountains behind her. I stood there, marveling. Dorothy's eyes filled with tears. "What's the matter?" I asked halfheartedly. She shook her head but didn't answer. She is a small, pale-faced child with large, pale blue eyes and long, pale brown hair. Everything about her is pale. She sat there against the trees and the sky, against the mysterious white mists rising on the mountains, and all she did was cry.

I looked at her helplessly. She seemed so unappealing. "What's wrong?" I tried again, but again she only shook her head.

Jerry came down the stairs from the sleeping

balcony, and we both considered Dorothy. "She's going to be a handful," I whispered.

Jerry moved over to Dorothy, sat down next to her and put an arm around her. "What is it, Dorothy?" he asked.

Dorothy shook her head, but Jerry pulled her closer. "Do you miss your mother? Is that it?"

Dorothy took her finger out of her mouth and began wailing. Jerry pulled her up on his lap and rocked her back and forth.

"You'll be fine, Dorothy," he crooned. "You'll see."

"No, no, no," yelled Dorothy, kicking her feet and gasping. "I wanna go ho—o—ome."

"You're going to have fun here," said Jerry. "Maybe we'll all go swimming later. Would you like that?"

"No, no, no—I want my mama. I need my mama."

"If we go swimming, we can play Rocked in the Cradle of the Deep. Did you ever play Rocked in the Cradle of the Deep?"

"I *need* my mama."

"Why do you need your mother?"

Dorothy put up her pale, puffy, wet face and whispered something in Jerry's ear.

"Is that all? Well, you go get your comb and brush, and Gloria will fix your hair and make you two beautiful braids just like your mama does."

"No," yelled Dorothy, "I don't want Gloria to fix my hair. I only want *you*."

"But I don't know how to make braids. I never fixed a girl's hair before."

Dorothy yelled until he said he would. Then she ran and got her comb and brush, and wouldn't let anybody else—not me, not even Mrs. Horne—fix her hair. Only Jerry.

So he had to do it while the rest of us stood around watching. I raised one eyebrow and looked towards Roger. He saw it and grinned. "Hey Jerry," he yelled, "when you finish with Dorothy you can set my mother's hair in the latest style, and then maybe you can work on the other girls."

The other boys picked it up and began laughing and teasing him. Jerry's face grew redder and redder as they laughed but he kept working on Dorothy's hair until he had made two lopsided, misshapen braids. Then Dorothy ran to her room and came back with two pink ribbons for him to tie at the ends of her braids.

"Oh pink," simpered Roger, sashaying around the room and talking in a high, phony girl's voice. "My favorite color!"

I laughed along with the rest of them, enjoying Jerry's humiliation and hating him for knowing how to handle Dorothy when I did not.

Chapter 6

July 10, 1943: Dorothy was crying again.

"Go on! Go on!" Roger shouted at Jason.

Jason hesitated. He stood on the plate, the ball in his hand, frozen.

Dorothy was crying loud. Her whine rose into a high screech. From the playing field nobody could see her but it sounded as if she was out on the back porch, probably hanging over the railing, directing her yells our way.

"Go on!" Roger waved his arms impatiently from second base.

"Why did you have to go and shout at her?" Fred demanded. "Now she'll tell her mother, and we'll all get it."

"Who cares!" Roger yelled. "Let's get on with

the game. Come on, Jase, are you going to stand there forever?"

Jason came alive. He turned his body sideways, and as he rocked back and forth on his legs, Roger took a few steps off second base, leering over his shoulder at Susie. Jason threw the ball up in the air with his left hand and punched it hard with his right. The ball snapped through the air, and Roger flew off towards third base.

I caught it easily and came running in to tag Roger on his way back from third. Two easy outs!

"You jerk!" Roger yelled at Jason. "Why did you hit it to *her*?"

"I didn't mean to hit it to *her*," Jason said.

"You could have hit it to Susie or even Bobby, but no—every time you get up, you hit it to *her*."

Her is me, Gloria. Every time somebody says *her* like that, the rest of them know without a doubt who it is. After only a week, I have become the acknowledged best at punchball—better than Jerry (Yah! Yah! Yah!), better than Roger, better than Andrea, better than Fred, better than Susie, better than Bobby, better than Jason, better than Dorothy. Sometimes I find myself chanting it— "Better than . . . better than . . . better than . . ." Nobody questions that I am the best. It gives me a prickly feeling at the roots of my hair, and I have to work very hard to keep the glory and triumph out of my face whenever somebody says *her*.

"I didn't want to do it," Jason protested, his

chubby face struggling to hide the pain. "I try but . . ."

"Oh you! You try . . . sure . . . you . . . !"

Dorothy's shrieks grew piercing.

Jerry began walking towards the house.

"Where are you going?" Roger shouted. "You're up next."

"I think your mother went to the greengrocer," Jerry said over his shoulder.

"Well, so, okay, she'll get over it. Come on back! Jerry!"

But Jerry kept going, not even bothering to reply.

"Oh darn that kid!" Roger swore. He was angry, and he looked around for a place to focus the anger. Jason was still standing there, so Roger pointed his finger at him but before he could say anything, Andrea turned and began walking towards the house too.

"Where are *you* going?" he yelled.

"To the house. I don't want to play anymore."

"Why not?"

"Because you're impossible." Andrea stopped and looked right at him. "You're such a sore loser."

"Who's a sore loser?"

"And you yell at everybody."

"Who yells?"

"Not only on the other team, but on your team too. That's why your team always loses—because you're always shouting at everybody."

She waited for Roger to answer but he just stood there looking at her, kicking the earth with his toe.

Andrea was wearing a dark blue tee shirt with a pair of white shorts. Her dark skin looked very dark against the white shorts.

"You demoralize your teammates."

Roger frowned, and in spite of my deep sympathy for him, I had to keep myself from laughing out loud. Andrea knew so many big words that Roger didn't. She was forever demoralizing him.

"I wish you wouldn't pick me. I don't mind punchball. As a matter of fact, I like it, but if you don't mind, just remember I don't want to be on your team—*ever*. Understand?"

She raised her eyebrows, cocked her head, and appeared to be waiting for an answer. When none came, she nodded at the rest of us—the queen dismissing her court—and walked off.

"I only pick her," Roger explained after she left, "because she can catch anything. She's not much of a hitter. I don't need her—stuck-up show-off! I'll show her. I'll never pick her again."

I came in from the outfield and sat down on the grass. Dorothy's cries were still high and shrill. "You shouldn't have shouted at her," I said kindly —Roger really was my favorite. "That started the whole thing. Now we can forget about playing for the rest of the morning."

Roger flung himself down next to me, and then Bobby, Fred, Susie and Jason came and sat down too. For a moment it was absolutely still, empty of human sounds. Warm sun on our backs—later it would grow warmer, and we would go swimming. Later we would walk down the road and through the little forest, fragrant with its floor of pine needles, to the stream. Now we sat so quietly that the silence began to hum and buzz around us. Then Dorothy shouted, "No!" and a soft voice, Jerry's voice, answered.

"Why did she have to come anyway? She's only five. She spoils everything," Roger said bitterly.

"Never mind," I comforted. "Tomorrow I'll take her on my team." Since Roger and I were the best players, we were always team captains.

"It's not fair—and Jerry, he jumps every time she hollers. He's got no backbone. Why doesn't he tell her off once in a while instead of always spoiling our games?" Roger began a whole string of grievances. His nose turned up at the bottom, and his blue eyes were intense.

He'll be handsome when he grows up, I thought, nodding at what he was saying, but not really listening. For the moment I had no part in Roger's suffering even though he was my favorite. On the punchball field I rarely suffered. Whoever was winning or losing, I was the best. Better than . . .

Better than Jerry! Better than Jerry in getting along with Roger! Better than Jerry in getting along with the other boys too! They liked me better, respected me more. I was stronger than all of them—even Roger, though he was just as tall.

Whenever we wrestled, I could always pin him to the ground, sooner or later.

"Oh! Oh! Oh!" Mrs. Horne said one day when she saw us twisted around each other on the ground. Later she said I might get hurt, tussling with the boys. "They don't know how girls are put together." She meant because I had breasts, though she didn't say so.

I couldn't tell her that girls with size 30 breasts didn't have to worry. I was as strong as any boy there, and it was glorious feeling the power flow through me as I overcame them one by one. I wasn't just a girl—I was a force.

Only Jerry refused to wrestle. He said he had a trick knee but I think he knew I could pin him down—the coward. He was better with Dorothy and Andrea than I was. Every morning he fixed Dorothy's hair, and lately he and Andrea read poetry to each other in the evenings. I despised them, resented them and was jealous of them.

Guiltily I focused in on Roger, wondering if he could sense what I was thinking, but he was so busy complaining, all he could think about were his own concerns. Besides, he couldn't read my mind. Nobody could. Inside my head, I could say anything I pleased—say that Andrea was a stuck-up little bitch, and Dorothy a spoiled repulsive brat, and Jerry a cowardly sissy, and Jason a loser who always managed to fly out to me. I giggled softly.

"What's funny?" Roger paused in the midst of his grievances, a hurt, suspicious look in his eyes.

"Nothing, nothing."

"My mother should have said no. Who needs a baby like that around?"

"Never mind!"

I lay back on the grass, and Roger continued complaining. Every so often, Dorothy would yell, "No!" or "Go away!" The grass was itchy and high; high above me, curly clouds moved slowly through a blue sky. I thought to myself, I'm really here. This is really happening to me.

This morning a letter came from my mother.

Dear Gloria,

You sure are lucky to be away in the country. For four days in a row, the temperature's been over 90. Herby started wheezing again, and last night he had to sleep up on the roof, he could hardly breathe.

The fan broke down at work, and one of the girls, Lily Kronberg—you might remember her. She was the big, fat one who brought you a little beaded purse on your tenth birthday. Anyway, she fainted.

In such terrible weather, Joe had to bring Bonny and her parents over two nights ago for coffee and cake. I wasn't even dressed when they came, and I had to hurry up and put some clothes on. I don't like it when people drop in on me, even though they brought a big, gooey chocolate cake. Who even wants to eat something like that in this weather?

Anyway, nothing new to report. I received your card, and I'm glad you arrived safe. Write soon, and let me know if you have enough clothes. Joe and Herby send their love.

Your loving,
Mother

It was a letter from my mother, but it came from another planet.

After dinner, Roger and Bobby had K.P. I took my book and hurried upstairs. Everybody tried to sit in the one creaky rocker on the back porch, and it was simply a matter of getting there first. Jerry was already occupying it, Dorothy in his lap. On the steps close by, Susie and Fred were playing Steal the Old Man's Bundle.

"Tell me another Dorothy story," Dorothy said.

"I just told you one."

"I want another."

"I'll tell you another before you go to sleep."

"No, now! I want it now!"

"Later."

"NOW!"

Once upon a time, Jerry began, *there was a little girl named Dorothy who went for a walk in the forest.*

Ho, hum! I yawned, and sat down on one of the chairs at the far end of the porch.

"And along came a big, bad wolf," said Fred.

"Shut up, Fred!" said Dorothy.

And along came Fred, said Jerry.

Susie giggled, and put a queen over the queen in Fred's pile.

Susie was with him, said Jerry, *and she said to Dorothy, "How would you like to come with us deep into the forest?"*

"I don't want to go," Dorothy said.

"Yes, I'd like to go very much," said Dorothy. "Thank you for asking me."

I opened my book and tried to read. After a week, I had only arrived at page 67. In the city, I would have finished the book in a few days, but here there was never any time.

"We have found a mysterious stream," Fred told Dorothy. "It has magical powers, and anyone who bathes in it can be transformed into anything he likes if he knows the magic word."

Fred took in a seven, and then turned, listening, in Jerry's direction.

"What is the magic word?" asked Dorothy.

"We don't know," Susie said, "but if we can find a mossy rock under a great oak tree, the word will be hidden beneath it."

"I don't want Susie to say so much," Dorothy said. "I want to be the one who says everything."

"Let's go find it," said Dorothy, taking Susie's hand.

Fred went on ahead, parting the bushes and peering carefully into all the caves they passed on the way. Suddenly a strange noise, like the sounds of many coconuts banging together, reached their ears, and Susie cried, "What is it?"

"Stay back," said Fred, "while I have a look."

"Hey, how about a game of punchball?" Roger cried, banging out onto the porch. "We're finished with the dishes."

"Just a minute," Fred said. He was holding three cards in his hand, and had covered a two with another two but had forgotten to take it in. "Go on, Jerry, what was it?"

"Doesn't anybody want to play?"

Roger, Jason, Bobby and I went off to play, but it wasn't much fun with only the four of us.

"Jerry never wants to do anything with us," Roger complained. "My mother promised us a guy who'd play with us."

"Gloria plays with us," said Jason.

The admiration in their eyes was almost embarrassing.

"Come on, we'll wrestle," I told them. After I'd thrown each of them down on the ground several times, we played hide-and-go-seek; and after it grew too dark to see anything, we returned to the house.

Only Mrs. Horne and Jerry were sitting on the porch now, talking quietly together.

"Where is everybody?" Jason wanted to know.

"Dorothy's asleep, and Andrea is showing everybody how to make s'mores."

"What's that?"

"She read about them in a book. It's a combination of graham crackers, chocolate, and marshmallows toasted over a fire. Jerry just built a fire in the fireplace, and that's where they are."

"Well, why didn't you tell me?" Roger and the other two boys hurried into the house. I sank down on the steps, out of breath and angry at the sight of Mrs. Horne and Jerry together. There was an uncertain moment, and then Mrs. Horne inquired, "Have a nice game?"

"Fine."

"That's nice."

Nobody said anything during another uncertain pause. My jealousy had risen into my ears by now, and was pounding away in back of my temples.

"We were talking about Dorothy," Mrs. Horne said finally.

"Oh?"

"Yes. I was saying how I could see quite a change in her."

"Oh?"

"Yes. I think she's not the unhappy, mousy little thing she was a week ago."

"Mmm."

"She's also eating better and laughing more, and she does try to take part in things. Wasn't it cute how she pretended to swim this afternoon, and acted as if we couldn't see her little feet trotting along under the water?"

She and Jerry laughed, and I turned away, hiding my furious face in the darkness.

"Ma!" came a cry from inside. "Roger has all the chocolate and he won't give me any."

"I shall return," said Mrs. Horne.

Nobody spoke while she was gone. I didn't know what Jerry was doing, but I was busy thinking of all the different ways I'd like to eliminate him. I wanted to bury him up to his neck in sand, and have the red ants finish him off. I wanted to drown him in the stream, hang him from a tree, shove him off a cliff. And most of all, I wanted to know, before I finished him off for good, what had made those sounds of many coconuts banging together in his story.

Chapter 7

July 17, 1943: Whenever Dr. Horne comes, bed-
lam reigns. Today I was awakened by the most
hideous howls—not a reassuring sound first thing
in the morning. I was about to leap out of bed to
investigate, but then I remembered *he* was here
for the weekend, so I hid my head under the pillow and groaned. By and by the fury abated, and
it grew so quiet I became suspicious and worked
myself upstairs to check out the action.

He had them all out on the back porch chanting
Peter Rabbit in Latin. When he spotted me, he
insisted I join in. He is the kind of man who needs
an entire audience in order to be perfectly happy.

Dominus McGregor erat in suis manibus et
genibus et brassicas novellas serebat, sed

exsiluit et cucurrit ad Petrum agitans rastrum
et clamans, "Siste, fur!"

"We'll go on to bigger and better things," he
told us at breakfast. "If you learn *Peter Rabbit*,
maybe we'll tackle *The Bobbsey Twins* next, and
by the time I'm finished with you, you'll be able
to read all the dirty words written on the walls of
Pompeii."

"Eddie! Eddie!" scolded Mrs. Horne, but the
kids giggled and everybody wanted to sit near
him, even Roger and Jason, who generally knock
everybody over to sit near me.

I don't mind that, but I do mind the frantic
hysteria that begins when he arrives and doesn't
stop until he leaves. Everybody becomes super-
charged—voices grow louder, movement speeds
up, games grow wild and stupid.

Dr. Horne offered to give Susie boxing lessons
after breakfast.

"Get up your dukes," he shouted, trying to sound
like Jimmy Cagney. He put up his fists and
crouched low, looking at her with a twisted sneer
on his face.

Giggling, Susie also crouched, imitating his
stance.

"Come on! Come on!" yelled Dr. Horne, slowly
circling her, his eyes narrowed and glinting.
"Whatsamatter, kid? Chicken?"

Susie was laughing so hard, she could hardly
stand. She is easy to please. But then, as Dr.

Horne continued to circle, she suddenly rushed forward and began pounding at him with both fists. He let out a bloodcurldling yell as Susie continued to giggle and flail away at him with her fists. Dr. Horne screamed such a horrible, loud and piercing yell that for the moment I lost my bearings and looked around, expecting to see hundreds of windows opening in 'The Bronx. Dr. Horne dropped, moaning, to the ground and lay there, his face twisted in agony. Susie bounced up and down on his belly, and Dorothy and Jason rushed over, shouting, "Me! Me! Now me!"

Roger arrived with a rope, and all the kids tied Dr. Horne up. Even Andrea joined in, with him howling all the time. It was disgusting.

Mrs. Horne came into the room while all this was going on, shook her head at the din, and smiled at me. "He's like a one-man circus," she said proudly. How could she?

Later we went swimming. There is a small piece of road that we have to take on the way to the stream, and the heat today was so fierce that it melted the hot tar and turned it squishy under our feet as we walked along. Dorothy cried and said she was tired, so Dr. Horne and Jerry took turns letting her ride piggyback. That kid is such a brat! By the time we arrived, all of us were dripping with sweat.

Our swimming hole is cut out of rocks and pine forests. The water is always cold and so clear you can see down to the bottom. On one side a waterfall feeds the swimming area, and on another a huge boulder overhangs it. Underneath the boulder, the water is at its deepest, shaded and green.

There are two ways to get in—slowly, letting the icy water gradually touch each bit and piece of you. That is the coward's way. That is Jerry's way. Today he stood nervously, as usual, by the edge of the pool, his pink skin peeling all down his back. The other way is to plunge right in, and that is my way. Racing past Jerry, and splattering him with cold water, I plunged, feeling the icy shivers weaving up my body, mingling with the hot beads of perspiration. As the water closed over my head, I became one long, delicious shiver of cold. "Aaah!" I came up screaming, beating the water with my hands and feet. Jason, Roger and Bobby followed, and soon were howling around me. In and out we dove until our bodies became a part of the stream.

Everything rippled underneath—rocks and legs and patterns of sunshine moved with the water. There were living things underneath that still unnerved me. A fish brushed my fingers and I scrambled up, panicking at the other life that shared the water with me. Exhausted finally, I found myself under the overhanging boulder. The water was so deep there, I could see no bottom. But my feet found a shelf on the boulder, and I rested there, panting.

The three boys were tussling and shooting huge geysers of water sprays in all directions. Andrea, over near the little waterfall on one side of the pool, was doing a perfect crawl, slow and graceful, her brown arms dark against the water. Susie and Dorothy lay downstream in the shallow water, and the others, except Jerry, sunned themselves on the small sandy beach. Jerry still stood at the edge of the pool, waiting for his courage to catch up with him.

Dr. Horne rose and came to stand next to Jerry at the edge of the pool. Slowly he moved forward, stopping finally with the water up to his knees. His large, white, hairy belly overhung his blue trunks the way the boulder I stood under overhung the water. I couldn't help laughing at him.

"Come on, Dad," Roger yelled. "Come on in. We're waiting for you."

"Hold your horses," Dr. Horne grumbled. He bent over, splashed some water over his face and shoulders, shivered, hesitated, and stepped back a step or two.

"Brr, it's freezing!"

"Come on, Dad," Jason urged. "You take forever." He splashed some water in his father's direction.

"Now cut that out!" commanded Dr. Horne.

Roger splashed some water then and so did Bobby.

"Now you just stop that," Dr. Horne roared, but the three boys suddenly hurled themselves at him, on him, around him. He attempted to retreat but, outnumbered, at bay, he screamed threats and reproaches as they dragged him further and further into the water. I laughed and laughed and laughed.

"Now stop this minute or you'll be sorry," he roared at them. "I'm not kidding, Roger. Jason, get off my back or I'll break your neck! Aah!" He was down. The giant was down, and the three victors pushed and prodded at his great bulk.

In an explosion of spray, he was up again, sputtering and spouting, with the water streaming from his eyes, his nose, his mouth. "That's *it*! GET AWAY!" he roared, and the boys, suddenly alarmed, radiated out and away from his reach.

"I told you NO but you didn't listen. NO is NO!" He was shrieking at them as he moved back to the shore.

"But Dad, we were only kidding," a frightened Roger began.

"Aw Dad . . ." from Jason.

"Keep away from me or I'll kill you," roared Dr. Horne, fury stiffening his body.

I could see that people on the beach were looking at him, at us, at each other. What a spectacle of himself he was making! Only Mrs. Horne, stretched out on a towel in the sun, seemed oblivious.

Dr. Horne came struggling out of the water, and the boys, penitent, moved in closer to apologize.

"I'm sorry, Eddie," Bobby said.

Dr. Horne was standing on the shore now, and he turned to look at the three boys as they swam towards him. His face had purpled with anger, and he bared his teeth and snarled, "I told you over and over again . . ."

There, there, for all to see, I thought, the great Dr. Horne revealed in his true form—sorehead, bully, vile-tempered terrorizer of little boys. Why didn't Mrs. Horne look up? How could she ignore his loud, humiliating performance?

"Aw, Dad, don't be mad."

"Please, Dad, I'm sorry. I won't do it again."

He turned away from their pleas and began walking towards Mrs. Horne. Suddenly he spun around, and plunged swiftly back into the water. The boys, caught off guard, attempted flight, but he caught them all, one by one, and ducked them and tossed them and slammed them around while a mountain of spray mingled with their screams and laughter.

I was not prepared when he swam over, plucked me off my ledge, and ducked me under too.

"But why me? Why me?" I protested when I emerged, my mouth full of water. "What did I do?"

"You laughed," he said, picking me up and tossing me over his head.

I suppose it was fun after all. The kids loved it. Andrea pretended that she only wanted to keep swimming her fine, graceful crawl. But she came in closer and closer until Dr. Horne noticed her and slammed her around like the rest of us.

"No, no!" she yelled at first, and then, "Me too, me too!"

I suppose he is a one-man circus, as Mrs. Horne said. If you think of him as a clown, he probably has a few good points.

July 18, 1943: Dorothy's mother came for her this morning. Roger couldn't wait. He started looking out for her practically at daybreak. "Thank God!" he told me. "Now we'll be able to play punchball without her howling every time she misses." Which isn't completely fair. Dorothy only howls when somebody (usually Roger) yells at her.

Jerry brushed and combed her hair, and she handed him two green plaid ribbons to tie at the ends of her braids. I must say that he has become pretty good at his job after two weeks, and Dorothy's braids are no longer clumsy and mis-shapen. Rah! Rah! for Jerry. At last he's found his true calling.

When her mother came, Dorothy fell down on the floor and kicked her feet. "I don't want to go. I don't want to go," she screamed.

"But Dorothy," said her mother, "you told me you wanted to come home. Every time I talked to you on the phone—just last Wednesday, as a matter of fact—you cried and said you wanted to come home."

"I don't want to go home. I hate you. I hate you."

Dorothy rolled around on the floor, dirtying her

green-and-white playsuit. The bows on her braids came undone.

"But Dorothy, I made this trip all the way up here to get you."

Dorothy's mother is a small, pale, nervous woman. Most likely when she was five, she looked like Dorothy. Most likely when Dorothy grows up, she will look like her mother. Both of them resemble little white rats. Now Dorothy's mother stood watching Dorothy, her nose twitching in a worried way.

"Come here, Lila, and let's talk it over," said Mrs. Horne. The two of them walked out onto the back porch.

"Damn it," said Roger, "now my mother will probably let her stay."

Dorothy stopped thrashing around. She lifted her head up off the floor and looked out to the porch. Jerry knelt down and retied her ribbons.

Dorothy stayed.

Before leaving, Dorothy's mother gave Jerry and me two dollars apiece. "I know you're making Dorothy very happy, and I can't thank you enough. She's having such a good time. You're wonderful to give her so much attention."

She was talking to both of us but she really meant Jerry.

Dorothy's mother and Dr. Horne left for the city late in the afternoon. Now it feels like us again. After the kids were asleep, Mrs. Horne came down to the kitchen to talk. She often does when Dr. Horne isn't here. We made brown bread and sugar. (This was her favorite snack when she was a girl. She taught me how to make it. I am learning to eat brown bread this summer, along with things I never liked or tried before, like Swiss chard, broccoli, birch beer, sardines, peanut butter and sweet pickles. Take a piece of brown bread, spread it with butter and sprinkle brown sugar over it. Yum!) We sat at the table, eating and talking. I knew she was lonely, knew she missed Dr. Horne, but so what. He was gone and wouldn't return for another two weeks. Whoopee!

"How fast the summer is going," she said, wrinkling her face. I suppose she was trying to persuade herself that the two weeks ahead would fly. But it struck me like a whack in the head. Two precious weeks gone, two out of my nine—only seven to go, and then back to the city. Even with Jerry here, and in spite of Andrea and Dorothy, I don't want to go. I want to stay here forever, sleeping in my corner of the kitchen, eating brown bread and sugar, and playing punchball.

Earlier today, Dr. Horne came out in the middle of our morning punchball game, just as Roger and I were pushing each other back and forth. Roger had caught a ball that Andrea hit, bobbled it, and dropped it. But he still insisted she was out. Naturally I protested, and the pushing had just begun. It seldom went much further, although once I had knocked Roger down on the ground, and twice he had hurled himself at me, twisting my arm in a vain attempt to get a ball away from me.

"Roger! Gloria!"

It had not seemed shameful before he arrived, but then suddenly it did. I especially felt ashamed, remembering that I was fifteen and considered a counselor.

"Since when, Roger, do you fight girls?"

As if that had anything to do with it. Poor Roger never had a chance against me anyway.

"It's nothing," Jason told him. "They never really hurt each other. Nobody really hurts anybody."

"It doesn't matter," said Dr. Horne solemnly. "This is just a game, and if it makes people so angry that they act like savages, then maybe you'd better find another game."

He spoiled our game. For the rest of the morning, we played our calmest, politest, and most boring game ever.

But now he's gone, and Mrs. Horne and I sat together tonight, talking and eating brown bread and sugar. She never interferes with us during our games, never says do this or do that or you should have or you shouldn't have. She comes only when invited. She never intrudes.

I like to look up and see her watching me. She watches her boys too, and the other kids. I don't mind any of that (except when she watches Jerry) because I know I am special in her eyes. She talks to me in little snatches during the day because I am busy with the kids, but at night, after they have gone to bed, sometimes she comes down to my kitchen and then we really talk. She talks to me about herself, and I keep very still so she won't notice me too much and stop talking. She tells me about her girlhood, how she grew up shy and overweight. How she loved to read Robert Browning's poems (I will read him when I get back to the city), and how she and Dr. Horne used to read them to each other after they fell in love (I'm not so interested in this part). She tells me about her worries over her children, her concern about being an adequate teacher. She talks to me as if I were another adult and a friend—a woman friend.

Strange how I hate being a girl during the day —how I want to be myself, not just a girl. But at night, sitting and talking woman talk with Mrs. Horne, I don't mind being a girl.

So far we haven't talked about me at all. But there is time—seven weeks to go, most of the summer yet to enjoy. It isn't moving all that quickly. Only two weeks gone. What's two weeks? Two weeks out of my life. Where did they go? I want them back.

Chapter 8

July 22, 1943: Roger, Jason, and Bobby are for me. Andrea and Dorothy are for Jerry. Fred and Susie are floaters. Sometimes they're for me and sometimes they're for him.

Like now, they're for him because he got the bright idea of working up an entertainment program for this Saturday night when Bobby's mother and Andrea's parents arrive to visit their kids. Jerry found an old copy of Longfellow's poems among some books the Hornes have up here, and he's all excited about doing a dramatic reading from *Hiawatha*. He figured Andrea could narrate, Bobby would act Mondamin, the maize god, and Fred could be Hiawatha. Bobby refused, so Fred said he'd like to play Mondamin; and then, to my surprise, Roger offered to play Hiawatha.

All the kids want to be on the program now, except for Bobby. Jerry said he would work up something for Dorothy and Bobby, and he asked me if I could figure out an act for Susie and Jason. Naturally, he handed me the two kids who have the least amount of talent. Susie lisps when she talks, and Jason can't and won't sing. I could have said no, but I didn't want it to get back to Mrs. Horne. Finally, I thought up an idea for a dance. Jason complained a lot in the beginning, but I can always handle Jason. Now he's enjoying it, I think, even though he won't admit it.

All week long we have been rehearsing in the barn where the performance will take place. Rehearsals cut into our punchball games, which is a drag. Worse yet is how Jerry keeps asking for my opinion.

"What do you think, Gloria? Should we have the audience sitting up in the loft, looking down onto the stage? Or should we have everything on one level?

"How about the lighting? Mrs. Horne can give us six lanterns, and we have twelve flashlights. Do you think that's enough?

"What about the costumes for Hiawatha? Do you think we could get away with bathing suits?

"And what should we do about Bobby?"

Bobby was refusing to do anything. Not for the right reason—that he hated Jerry and wouldn't do anything to please him—but because he just didn't want to. He offered to be in charge of sound effects and lights.

"But your mother is coming up," Jerry explained. "She'll want to see you in something."

"No," Bobby said.

"You *have* to!" I told him finally. "And that's all there is to it. You just *have* to!"

Jerry smiled at me, and I turned away, annoyed. I don't like siding with him, ever, but in this instance, there was no choice. I don't expect it will happen again.

July 24, 1943: The performance was a flop, and the parents pretended to enjoy it very much.

Andrea was M.C. She started off by welcoming the audience—Mrs. Horne, her parents, Dr. and Dr. Fuller, and Bobby's mother, Mrs. Mason—to our summer theater. Then she introduced herself as the first performer, who would recite three poems by Nathalia Crane. She knew the poems by heart but pretended to read so that she could peer owlishly over the edge of the book and look patronizingly at the audience. Her voice, cold and crisp, made each word stand up and behave itself. She is too frosty for my tastes.

> In the darkness, who would answer
>   for the color of a rose,
> Or the vestments of the May moth
>   and the pilgrimage it goes?

In the darkness who would answer,
in the darkness who would care,
If the odor of the roses and the
winged things were there.

When she got to the word *odor*, Roger looked at me and held his nose. We were peering down from the loft, watching the performance (the audience was down on the ground level), and I had to stuff some straw in my mouth to keep from laughing out loud. Roger hates and resents Andrea, but I think if she were nicer to him, he could really like her.

She read three poems and, of course, the audience applauded enthusiastically. Gravely she acknowledged their applause by nodding kindly several times before moving off behind a post.

After a moment or two, she returned to announce the next number—a dance entitled "The Fairy and the Elf," featuring Susie Rose and Jason Horne; choreography, costumes and sets by Gloria Rein. This was my debut as a choreographer, and I was suddenly experiencing stage fright. Nervously, I climbed down the ladder, and proceeded to arrange the sets, which consisted of a sprinkling of grass and some buckets of daisies to simulate a wooded glen. After directing a bashful grin at the audience, I then retired, hurried back up to the loft again, and poised over the portable record player. Susie, wrapped mostly in Mrs. Horne's scarves over her bathing suit, stood on one leg, watching me.

"Are you ready?"

"Yes."

"Go ahead."

Susie gracefully clambered down the ladder, and curled herself up into a gauzy ball on the floor as the audience murmured and applauded lightly. In my dance, Susie is a sleeping fairy who is discovered by an elf. He is enchanted by her and tries to awaken her, but she sleeps on. He dances around her, and at last leaps over her several times until she wakes up. From then on, Susie takes over the dancing, much to Jason's relief (and mine too). As the music ends, they dance off the stage together.

"Are you ready?" I whispered to Jason.

"Uh . . ."

I put the needle on the record, and as the strains of *The Nutcracker Suite* filled the room, Jason moved a little closer to me. He was dressed in an old pair of Roger's green swimming trunks, a cut up green-and-white striped apron of Mrs. Horne's, and a painted cardboard hat. His chubby face appeared green as well. "I'm scared," he whispered.

"Get moving," I hissed encouragingly. "There's your cue."

He lingered near me.

"Go!" I gave him a confident shove, feeling my own nervousness eating away at my insides. Activated by my shove, he lumbered off and climbed heavily down the ladder. Crazy boy, he'd forgotten to remove his shoes! Crazy me for not noticing it! The first part of the dance had him leaping over Susie's prostrate form, which he did with loud crunches and crashes. Susie could be seen to tremble after each leap, and the audience roared.

"You know what?" Andrea whispered to me. "This shouldn't be titled 'The Fairy and the Elf.' A better name for it would be 'The Fairy and the Elephant.'"

I could have murdered her and the audience too for clapping so loudly after my massacred dance ended. Susie and Jason were brought back for two curtain calls, but I refused to climb down when somebody yelled "Choreographer! Choreographer!"

The next disaster was Dorothy reciting "Lavender's Blue." Dressed all in pink—matching playsuit, ribbons, and socks—she emerged holding Jerry's hand. She stood there looking up at him while she recited in a high, quavery little voice.

> Lavender's blue, dilly dilly
> Lavender's green;
> When you are king, dilly dilly
> I shall be queen.
> Who told me so, dilly dilly
> Who told me so?
> 'Twas mine own heart, dilly dilly
> That told me so.

He kept feeding her the right words as she forgot them, and naturally he blushed throughout the whole performance. Even in the dim light everybody could see his cheeks flaming away. It was pitiful but again the audience clapped and clapped and clapped. Dr. Fuller even stepped forward and took a daisy from one of my pots and gave it to Dorothy. She immediately handed it to Jerry, whose cheeks by now should have melted from the heat.

But I had other concerns. Anxiously I listened as Andrea introduced the next number. This was Jerry's baby, and if it turned out better than mine, I'd be doubly humiliated. I needn't have worried.

"A dramatic rendition of 'Hiawatha's Fasting' from *The Song of Hiawatha* by Henry Wadsworth Longfellow," Andrea announced solemnly. "Roger Horne will act the part of Hiawatha, Fred Prince will be Mondamin, Andrea Fuller will be narrator. Jerry Lieberman, our producer and director, will provide the musical accompaniment.

Jerry brought out a stool for Andrea, gave her a flashlight to read by, and cleared my daisies off the stage. He then carried out something under a blanket and spread it down near Andrea. She began to read.

> You shall hear how Hiawatha
> Prayed and fasted in the forest,
> Not for greater skill in hunting,
> Not for greater craft in fishing,

> Not for triumphs in the battle,
> And renown among the warriors,
> But for profit of the people,
> For advantage of the nations.

Roger climbed down, barefoot, from the loft. Behind him, as appropriate background music, Jerry played something on the harmonica, something that sounded like a cross between the *Moonlight Sonata* and "Red River Valley." Roger was chewing gum; clearly, noisily chewing gum. I began to feel better. He continued chewing gum throughout the entire performance. From time to time Jerry paused in his harmonica playing to signal frantically to him, but Roger never looked at him. When Fred appeared as the god Mondamin, covered with corn husks, Roger was chewing. As they wrestled together, Roger chewed. Whatever Hiawatha was doing in the poem—

> He meanwhile sat weary waiting
> For the coming of Mondamin,

Roger chewed. All through the tragic scene of Mondamin's death and transfiguration into maize for the people, Roger chewed. As the stalk of corn gradually pushed its way up from Mondamin's grave (the blanket which covered Fred), and the grateful Hiawatha

Gave the first feast of Mondamin
And made known unto the people
This new gift of the Great Spirit

Roger chewed.

My spirits danced even through the numerous
curtain calls accorded the cast. I knew pity when
I saw it, and I had seen it earlier that evening
with my own fiasco, "The Fairy and the Elf."

The final number was Bobby's, and nobody, not
even me, knew what he planned on doing. He had
agreed to do *something* if he was allowed to practice in private. Now he hurried outside to prepare.
To my surprise, Andrea, after requesting the audience's patience for just a few minutes, followed
after him. We could all hear the sounds of giggling
and some clangings and bangings. Andrea and
Bobby? I frowned, not approving that one of my
followers was fraternizing with one of Jerry's.

Andrea returned finally and announced, "Our
final number this evening is a one-man band performance of 'Jingle Bells.'"

And here Andrea began singing "Jingle Bells"
and clapping her hands. We could hear Bobby
coming before we could see him. He burst through
the barn door and everybody laughed. Bobby was
covered with pots and pans that hung all over him.
He had a small washboard hanging down his front,
pot lids draped around his middle, and a long
string of cowbells looped around his neck and

shoulders. He nodded at Andrea, and she yelled,
"Now everybody sing," and everybody did.

> Jingle Bells! Jingle Bells!
> Jingle all the way!
> Oh, what fun it is to ride
> In a one-horse open sleigh-eigh!

Bobby marched around and around, jingling his
cowbells, beating his pot lids, clanging his pots
and pans, and drumming his washstand, while his
mother watched him proudly. He was the smash of
the evening. So much for the taste of the audience.

There was to be lemonade and cookies afterwards at the cast/audience party back at the house.
I helped Bobby dismantle and then had to listen
to his mother talking about how he inherited his
sense of humor from her side of the family.

By the time I got down to the kitchen to give
Mrs. Horne a hand with the refreshments, naturally Jerry was already there.

"Quite an evening!" she was saying. "You're
really a magician. Do you know that?"

"Me?" he said blushing, the hypocrite!

I moved up close to her, but she kept right on
talking to him. "Yes, you! Of course, you! That
Hiawatha was sheer inspiration."

"Even though . . ."

"Yes, yes, even though Hiawatha never stopped
chewing gum; and Dorothy was enchanting in
her little poem."

"Even though . . ."

"Even though you had to keep prompting her. The whole evening was a great success, and the kids adored it. That's what really mattered. They adored it, and they helped each other. Just look at Andrea, how much she enjoyed it, and just look at how good-natured she's become. Imagine her collaborating with Bobby!"

"They're all great kids," Jerry said, "they really are!"

Mrs. Horne hugged him hard; then she turned to me, smiling.

"I was just telling Jerry what an enchanting evening it's been, and I think you . . ."

"Yes, I heard you," I told her coldly, and left the two of them to bring up the refreshments themselves.

Chapter 9

July 26, 1943: He crowds me, breathes down my back, stands in my sunshine.

Even the housework. I tried to make it very clear to Mrs. Horne that I was not going to be exploited just because I was a girl. I am certainly willing to do my share, but I want the rest of them, especially Jerry, to do theirs too. Just because I'm a girl doesn't mean that I have to do more dishes, make more beds, sweep more floors than anybody else. I am willing to be part of a schedule—work it out scientifically—i.e., if I do the dinner dishes Tuesday, he should do them Wednesday. If I sweep the kitchen Saturday, he should do it Sunday. Write it out—fair and square.

But no—he jumps all the time. He's done more dishwashing than I, swept more floors, made more beds, braided more braids, sliced more carrots, carried out more garbage. . . . He's trying to show me up, make me look like a shirker.

Nothing I do upsets him. Every morning he continues to fix Dorothy's hair, and even my open contempt and Roger's teasing don't shake him much. And his stories—his silly, stupid stories! He has made a whole new underground kingdom now underneath that rock in the forest. All the children have adventures there—all the ones that listen. They are no longer Dorothy stories but Dorothy, Fred, Susie, Andrea and even Jason stories. Only Roger, Bobby and I refuse to listen.

July 27 1943: We were walking back from our punchball game this morning when Andrea cried, "Look!" She moved up close to me and held on to my arm. Even with the breath of her fear hanging over me, I was aware that she had taken my arm, that she had looked to me for protection.

"What? Where?" I said.

"There!" She pointed to a shuddering clump of grass under a tree.

"Maybe it's a snake," Bobby yelled, moving up closer to me. To me! It gave me courage.

"Stay here!" I ordered the two of them, and took a step forward. Snakes were still scary to me, but I'd seen several since the summer began, and knew that I could run faster than they could.

A robin lay thrashing in the grass, its throat torn and bleeding.

"What happened?" Susie cried.

"Maybe some animal caught it, and we just scared it away."

The robin lay on its back, helplessly twisting and turning.

"Well, we have to do something," I said. "Jason, go inside and bring me a needle and thread, some Mercurochrome, and a pair of scissors. We'll operate."

I picked the bird up in my hands and felt it feebly beat its wings in panic. I tried to stroke its head and its breast, to comfort it with friendly fingers, but its body twisted in terror in my hands.

"Poor thing," I murmured. "Don't be afraid." I laid it down on the ground and asked Andrea to hold its head steady while I operated. First I swabbed its throat with Mercurochrome; then I puckered the skin of its neck together and quickly stitched it up. The robin struggled feebly all the time I was working on it. I tried to move quickly, to speak encouragingly to it, to make it understand I was trying to help. I felt its warm blood on my fingers, and I knew that I stood between it and death. I worked quickly, and when I finished, the bleeding had stopped and the robin lay still—I hoped sleeping—on the ground.

I held it in my hand, and felt the faint beating of its heart against my fingers.

"Live! Live!" I willed.

I looked up to see Jerry leaning against a tree, his face pale for a change.

"What's wrong with you?" I cried. The robin lay warm but silent in my hands.

"I . . . uh . . . I think . . . I'm going to faint."

"Faint?"

Dorothy ran over and took his hand.

"Do you want a drink of water, Jerry?" Andrea called.

My fingers cradled the bird. How strong I was, compared to Jerry. "Poor little sissy," I murmured, "can't stand the sight of blood! Poor baby!"

Jerry's cheeks turned even paler, and he held on tightly to the tree. He looked like a drunk, and I laughed out loud. Roger began laughing too, and then, one by one, all the children laughed at Jerry —even Andrea. Even Dorothy. He clung to the tree, and we all stood there laughing.

"Jerry!" Mrs. Horne came from behind us. She moved swiftly to Jerry, made him sit down, made him bend his head into his lap, and crouched beside him, saying soothing things. Soon he was able to stand, and we watched as she helped him into the house. She did not look at me.

We found a box, lined it with grasses, and put the robin inside. Dorothy wanted to cover it with a little doll blanket, but I persuaded her to go with Fred and dig up some worms in case the robin wanted something for supper.

We brought the robin into the house, and laid it on the window seat. All through the evening it received continual nursing care as each of us, except Jerry, took turns attending it.

"Look! Look! His wings are fluttering," cried Susie.

"Should we try to give him some water from a dropper?" Roger asked.

"Should we cut up some worms for him?" asked Dorothy.

They asked me, for I was their leader, their chief of staff, their head surgeon. Nobody wanted Jerry.

"Just let him sleep," I advised, and they obeyed, tiptoeing as they approached the patient, and speaking in worried whispers.

All evening long the vigil continued, but at 8:30, the robin died.

"You did everything you could for him," Andrea comforted. "He had the best possible care."

We buried him by moonlight where we found him, beneath the chestnut tree. Dorothy scattered daisies and clover on his grave, and Fred found a flat rock for a tombstone. On it, Andrea wrote:

> *Here lies a robin*
> *Dead before his time*
> *Gone from this earth*
> *To a fate more sublime*
>
> *R.I.P. July 27, 1943*

July 28, 1943: Nothing much has changed. This morning Jerry brushed and combed Dorothy's hair, popped out twice at punchball and blushed

bright red when Roger cursed at home plate.
Things are back to normal except I know she's
mad at me. Tonight she didn't come down to eat
brown bread and sugar with me. Grown-ups—even
Mrs. Horne—can make a perfectly natural event
become shameful. So what if I teased Jerry? So
what if the kids laughed at him? What harm did it
do?

July 29, 1943: When she didn't come down tonight, I went upstairs. Everybody else was asleep,
but there was a crack of light under her door. I
tapped very lightly, and she said, "Come in."

She was reading in bed, propped up against her
pillows, her wonderful gray and black curly hair
like a broken halo around her face. She is not a
pretty woman—her skin is too sallow, and her eyes
too small. But the bones in her face are beautiful
—her high cheekbones give her an exotic, mysterious look. Her eyes narrowed as I entered. She
looked like a cat.

"Yes?"

She wasn't making it easy for me.

"I wanted to say I'm sorry."

"For what?"

"For making fun of Jerry." There now, it was
out. I felt better already. I smiled helplessly at her,
waiting for her approval.

"It's not enough."

"What?"

"Being sorry. It's not enough doing a cruel,

hurtful thing, and then saying you're sorry after. It's too late—the harm has already been done."

"But he's all right. He's forgotten it. He's talking to me, and none of the kids are ribbing him about it anymore. It's all over."

"I'm not talking about him."

"Well then—who?"

"I'm talking about you, Gloria. You're the one who's been hurt and diminished. You've attacked somebody when he was powerless to help himself. You've taken an ugly step. How far will it lead you?"

My anger blazed inside me. "You only care about him, not me. You like him better. You think he's a better person."

"Yes I do," she said calmly.

"You think the kids like him better too."

"Some of them do, yes. . . ."

"Better with the chores."

"No question."

"Better natured."

"Absolutely."

"Patient, kind, reverent and clean," I roared.

"Usually . . ."

"I hate him," I yelled, and stamped my feet. When I looked towards her, she was smiling. "And I hate you too."

I kicked her bed, and she said, "Gloria! Gloria!" and suddenly I was in her arms.

"Oh, Mrs. Horne," I wept, and snuggled up against her as if I was a little child. There was a warmth and a smell about her, a mother smell, that I'd nearly forgotten.

"I can't help it," I moaned. "I hate him. I hate him. I hate him. He's a sissy, a soft, spoiled sissy."

She patted my hair, and she began talking. "You hate him because he's different, but you're different too. You don't want anybody to lock you inside of being a girl. You want to be strong and independent and free. You want to be yourself. Why should you despise him for also wanting to be free? He doesn't want to be locked inside of being a boy either. He wants to be himself."

"He's weak and cowardly."

"And he's kind and patient and understanding. Why should you hate him so much?"

I told her. "Because you *made* him assistant editor of *Wings* with me. Because you like him better than me. Because . . ."

"I never said I liked him *better* than you—but Gloria, there are people I do like . . . I love . . . better than you. Does that mean you will have to hate everybody I love?"

"Not Roger or Jason," I muttered. "I'd never hate them."

"Of course not," she said, disregarding my omission of Dr. Horne's name. "You can't ever like all the people your friends like, but watch out for hatred. It hurts the hater much more than the hated."

"He's talented too," I cried. "It's not fair. He doesn't suffer at all. You're supposed to suffer if you're talented—especially if you're a poet. It's not fair."

"How do you know he doesn't suffer?"

"I just know."

"Because on the surface you see a kind, good-natured boy who has many friends?"

"And whose family thinks he's the greatest."

"It doesn't mean that he doesn't have disappointments and pain like most people."

"He wants to be handsome like his horrible brother, Sanford, and he doesn't want to blush. He told me so himself."

"And I imagine there are many things he didn't tell you. But, Gloria, what do you want?"

"I want . . . I want to be editor-in-chief of *Wings*."

"And what makes you think that's a worthier ambition than being good-looking?"

"You're disappointed in me," I whined. "You think I'm no good."

"You're very good," she said, smiling. "You make everything an epic experience. Even punchball becomes an Olympic event when you play. The kids—especially the boys—adore you. You make them feel larger than life, and that's wonderful. You're also strong and decisive—look how you tried to save the robin. I think you're compassionate too. You cared about the bird—but at the same time your jealousy made you attack Jerry. It's a better world, Gloria, if you let your compassion grow bigger than your jealousy. It's a bigger world too, you'll find, with lots of room for both you and Jerry."

July 30, 1943: I apologized to Jerry this morning. He didn't say it was too late, the way Mrs. Horne did. He said, "What for?"

"Because I made fun of you the other day when you felt faint because of the bird."

Jerry winced. "The sight of blood always makes me faint." There he was, blushing again. I looked away and concentrated on keeping my eyebrows from rising. "Once I actually fainted when my sister, Myra, cut her finger, slicing bread. It's disgusting."

"Never mind," I told him. "The smell of fish always makes me want to throw up."

"It's not the same."

"Well, anyway, I'm sorry."

"For what?"

July 31, 1943: Tonight Jerry put me in his story. It was really a Jason story, but for the first time everybody was listening to it. We all were on the back porch, just before Dorothy's bedtime, and even after the darkness hid our faces from one another, and the mosquitoes started biting, we all stayed there until Jerry finished his story. It was a long, long one about Jason questing for a silver key that opens all doors. In the course of his travels he met all of us—Dorothy, Andrea, Bobby, Susie, Roger, Fred and finally me. Everybody helped him with advice or supplies, but I helped him the most because I gave him a magic needle and thread. With it, he was able to sew up time and never grow old until his quest was completed.

I could use a magic needle and thread myself to sew up my jealousy. The story was very beautiful, but I couldn't help wishing I was the one who told it.

Chapter 10

August 2, 1943: In the mornings, Jerry always combs and brushes Dorothy's hair right after breakfast. Jerry sits on the window seat upstairs in the living room, and Dorothy stands in front of him. First he unbraids her braids, and then he brushes and brushes until all the snarls are out.

Dorothy's hair reaches down to her behind. More and more it occupies the attention of the other kids.

"Let me do it a little," Susie begged this morning.

"No!" said Dorothy.

"Let me," offered Andrea.

Dorothy didn't object, so Andrea picked up the brush and began working away. After it had been brushed for a while, Dorothy's hair lay smooth and soft and shining all around her like a great veil. It is beautiful hair—a fine, silvery brown with delicate curling edges and soft curly wisps. What a pity that under that spectacular hair stands only Dorothy.

"Give me a chance," pleaded Jason. "I never get a chance."

"No," said Dorothy.

"How about me, Dorothy?" Bobby smiled his special, disarming smile.

"Well . . ."

"Come on, Dorothy. You know I'm your friend. Didn't I show you how to do the dead man's float yesterday?"

"Well, all right, but don't press hard. Last time you pressed too hard."

Very carefully, Bobby drew the brush down the back of Dorothy's hair. Very gently, he moved the brush in long, careful swipes.

"Now it's my turn," said Roger.

Dorothy stood beaming in the midst of all the attention. She bestows her favors on her friends and denies them to her enemies. The lists change from day to day, but every morning at least three or four of the kids participate in Dorothy's hair-brushing rite.

Only me. I never do. I want to but I'm afraid she'll say no if I ask. In the beginning, I couldn't stand Dorothy and I guess she felt the same way about me. It's different now. I have nothing against her, and I love her hair. When I watch the kids brushing it with long, graceful swoops, my arms almost ache.

Every morning I think maybe I'll ask today. Maybe I'll just say it casually—maybe laughing. Maybe something like "Well, I guess I may as well have a turn too," or "We might as well make it a hundred percent membership." But what if she says no? What if she wrinkles up her nose, shakes her head and just says no? What then?

I could ask Jerry to let me do it one morning. He'd say yes. I know he'd say yes. It wouldn't matter to him at all, but then I'd owe him a favor. I can't take anything from him without giving him something back.

August 3, 1943: I didn't have to ask him. He just knew I wanted to do it. Today he saw me watching. I guess the hunger was written all over my face, and he just held the brush out to me and said, "Here, Gloria, you do it for a while."

Dorothy stiffened. I could see her stiffen. She looked at me, considering. I tried to look nonchalant but agreeable. I tried to keep the desire out of my face. She leaned against Jerry and then put up her face, whispering something in his ear.

"Of course I'll make the braids. After Gloria brushes, I'll make them. Okay?"

"Okay."

He handed me the brush, and I took his seat. Dorothy stood before me, her face turned the other way. All I saw was her wonderful hair, and carefully, respectfully, I began brushing. I could feel the silky softness against my hand. Nothing seemed more important than moving my arm up and down, up and down. I hadn't ever brushed anybody's hair before, and I almost wanted to cry. Up and down, up and down.

After a while, I became aware of the head that lay under all that hair, and the small, thin body that stood before me. When Jerry brushes her hair, she sometimes leans back against him, but now, with me, she stood up straight and as far away as she could. I wondered what she would do if I put an arm around her and pulled her closer to me. If I settled her against my leg, or even pulled her into my lap. I'd never noticed before how small a child she was. Should I? Shouldn't I? Should? But before I could, Dorothy said, "Come on, Jerry, make my braids *now*." Maybe next time.

August 4, 1943: Today I paid back my favor to Jerry. We were out in front of the house this afternoon, waiting for the others to come swimming. Roger and I were wrestling, and Jerry, Dorothy and Fred were sitting on the steps, watching. I had Roger in a headlock, and was concentrating on weakening his stance when Jerry called out, "Get your feet wider apart, Roger. Your balance will be better."

Of course, Jerry was right, and it took me longer to throw Roger than it should have.

"You have to concentrate on your balance," Jerry advised. "That's your real weakness."

"Baloney," grumbled Roger as I helped him up. "She's just too strong for me."

"But if you stood more carefully . . ."

"Let's see *you* try," said Roger.

"Go ahead," Fred chimed in. "You never do."

"My knee . . ." Jerry began, but the others kept urging him. Even Dorothy said, "Go on, Jerry, push Gloria down."

So there he was, standing in front of me, blushing bright red, and blinking nervously. We got our feet together and began.

Jerry is a couple of inches taller than me and heavier. I hooked one arm through his, and around his back. There is a lot of meat on his back, and my arm traveled quite a distance before it could fasten on an edge. This is real, I thought. He is bigger and stronger than all the little boys here. I am contending with the genuine article. I could feel the juices flowing inside me, and I willed myself to win. Better than . . . better than . . . better than!

"Oops, I'm sorry," Jerry apologized. I don't know why. Maybe his fingers closed on something unfamiliar. If he was going to waste time worrying about my being a girl, he would only be putting himself at an even greater disadvantage.

I pressed my shoulder into his chest and, crouching, heaved against him. His hands began tightening on my shoulder, around my waist.

"Oops, I'm sorry."

"Come on, Jerry," Dorothy hollered. "Push her down and let's go swimming."

There was no real hardness to him, but he had me in sheer bulk and weight. Maybe he even weighed twenty or thirty pounds more than I. I'm wiry and bony but quick and very strong. I shoved hard into him, and tried to press my knee into the back of his. Impossible to budge him! Unless I could get him off balance, I'd never throw him. I moved around to his other side, weaving my arms around his chest. I moved my arm up around his neck and his hands brushed across my chest.

"I'm sorry."

I pressed my knee into his, and he staggered. I had him! I had him! Quickly I caught him around the neck from behind, and pulled him backwards. He staggered, and I could feel the whole bulk of him beginning to collapse. I was playing Hiawatha to his Mondamin.

And the more they strove and struggled,
Stronger still grew Hiawatha

But I let him go—just eased up on my hold— and he regained his balance, shook off my arm, and turned to face me. I had him. He knew I had him. He knew I could have thrown him and he knew I'd purposely let him go. I was saying thank you for Dorothy. I was paying him back.

Mrs. Horne, Andrea and Susie came out on the

steps, and we went off swimming. We never did
finish our wrestling match. I don't think we ever
will. To the kids, it looked like a draw, and I'm
willing to leave it there. I could have thrown him
but I didn't. It's enough that we both know it.

August 5, 1943: Jerry came downstairs to my
kitchen tonight. Mrs. Horne has a cold and went
to bed early.

"Usually I'm out like a light," he said, "but
tonight I couldn't sleep. I've been sitting outside
in front of the house, and I've seen four shooting
stars." His voice was high with excitement.

"No kidding!" I said politely.

"They're beautiful. Would you . . . I mean . . .
would you like to come out and watch? Nobody
else is up. I mean . . . if you're busy . . ."

I was sitting in my bunk reading and half doz-
ing, but his invitation caught me off guard. "No,
that's okay," I told him, climbing down from my
bunk and putting on my bathrobe. "I'm just looking at my book. I haven't gotten very far with it—
only up to page 157. I keep falling asleep over it."

"I haven't even gotten that far with mine. Come
on, then. It's perfect outside."

We sat out in front of the house, looking up. The
stars crowded the sky, swarmed all over it, unlike
the city skies that seem so much more roomy. All
around us, fireflies flashed on and off. Nothing happened.

"Keep watching," Jerry urged.

I craned my neck and watched. Nothing happened.

"I swear there were four or five right in a row," Jerry said. "I wasn't even watching for them."

"That's always the way it is."

"Let's just watch a little longer. Are you cold?"

"A little, but it's okay. The sky is beautiful even without any shooting stars."

"Yes, isn't it? I love it here. I'm not even homesick anymore."

"Oh? Were you homesick?"

"Sure I was. I thought you noticed. I tried hiding it from the kids—especially Dorothy and Bobby. They were so terribly homesick themselves."

"Bobby? Bobby was homesick?"

"Especially Bobby."

"I never knew that," I said stiffly.

"Well, maybe because you're not sleeping with him . . . I mean . . ."

The darkness hid his cheeks, which must have been flaming.

". . . he used to cry at night."

"You mean all the boys *knew* he was homesick?"

"Sure they did. I had to sit on his bed some nights, and talk to him until he fell asleep."

"They never said anything to *me*. Bobby never said anything."

"Well, you know everything looks brighter in the daytime. Besides, I guess he'd feel funny about telling *you*."

"Why? Why wouldn't he want to tell me?"

"Because you're so . . . brave yourself."

Were his cheeks bright red when he said that? I knew they were, and I looked hard at the sky, embarrassed. Was I brave? So brave that a homesick boy couldn't tell me he was homesick? And if he had, what would I have done?

"But he's over it, and so am I. I used to write letters home every day, and wait for the mail as if it was the high point of the day. Now I write maybe a couple of times a week and sometimes I even forget to read my letters until the next day."

"You get a lot of letters."

"Some are from my friends."

"You must have a lot of friends."

"I don't know. I guess you never feel you have enough friends. Do you?"

"I don't have any friends."

"You don't?"

"No. People don't like me."

"That's not true, Gloria. Lots of people like you and admire you."

"Like who?"

"Like . . . me. I've always liked you and admired you."

Now I could feel my face very warm against the night air. Were my cheeks as red as his?

"I don't know why, Jerry. I never liked you."

"I know that, and . . . I'm sorry."

"What are *you* sorry about?" I hissed at him. "*I'm* the one who's sorry. Do you think I like feeling this way all the time? Do you think I like being jealous of you? Yes, that's right—jealous of you, and angry too. I'm angry because Mrs. Horne made you assistant editor, and I'm jealous because you're good, and she knows it, and I know it. That's why I've been such a stinker all summer. It's not your fault, so stop being sorry. I know it's my fault, and I'm sorry, but I'm jealous all the same. I keep trying to like you, Jerry, but it's not easy."

Now it became so quiet that I was suddenly aware of the crickets. I kept my eyes fastened on the sky, and waited.

"Is there anything I can do?" He sounded as if he was talking to a sick person. I burst out laughing.

"Don't you ever get angry?"

"Sure I do. Everybody does."

"I mean . . . I've been such a stinker all summer. I've been nasty to you, and I've made fun of you and teased you. Aren't you angry?"

"No—not at you."

"Why not? Why not at me?"

"It doesn't matter; but Gloria, listen Gloria, if you wanted, you could have lots of friends. You don't realize how many people like you—just look at Roger and Jason and . . ."

"Dorothy doesn't like me."

"Oh, Dorothy! She would if you spent a little time with her."

"And Andrea doesn't . . ."

"Everybody can't like everybody, but Gloria, when you're ready to have friends, believe me, you'll have them."

There wasn't a single shooting star in that whole blasted sky.

"I'm ready . . . I think," I said in a small, nervous voice.

We stayed watching for another fifteen or twenty minutes before we gave up and came inside. I showed Jerry how to make brown bread and sugar, and he ate five pieces. We stayed up eating and talking until after 2:30. In the morning, Jerry was crankier than I had seen him all summer long, but not me. I even played jacks with Susie, and wrote a long, not unpleasant letter home to my mother.

Chapter 11

August 7, 1943: Jerry refuses to say why he wasn't angry at me during the earlier part of the summer when I was so nasty to him.

"It doesn't matter," he keeps saying. But it does to me.

Jerry and I are friends. Yesterday he shouted at me during our punchball game and called me a cheater, but this morning he taught me to play "Barcarolle" on his harmonica. For the past two nights we have been watching for shooting stars. Tonight I finally saw one. Jerry's head was turned, and he missed it ripping across the sky. He has seen six or seven since the summer began, but I told him that mine was the best. Later, he, Mrs. Horne and I came down to the kitchen to schmooze. Even if she says nice things to him now, I don't mind—much.

I know now that Mrs. Horne will not change her mind and make me sole assistant editor. I even know that Jerry and I will have to go on and become coeditors-in-chief. Even though we are friends now, I still want the editorship all for myself. But I try not to think about it.

Which is easy up here. Every day is so full of summer. Fred and Susie are turning the barn into a nature museum. They go around collecting bugs and making up silly scientific-sounding names for them. Dr. Horne offered to bring up a bug book for them next weekend but they turned him down. Dorothy has been digging up worms in a damp spot down near the stream. She keeps them inside her pail and feeds them grass and clover. She talks to them the way Jerry talks to her, and tells them worm stories.

Bobby's mother brought him a fishing pole, and he's been trying to fish. Dorothy won't let him have any of her worms, and he has to dig up his own. So far he hasn't caught any fish, but every day while we're swimming he stands upstream, his pole in his hand, waiting.

August 13, 1943: Six weeks of the summer gone! I have even forgotten for almost a week now to write in my diary. This week has been the best.

But it didn't start that way. On Sunday, Mrs.

Horne offered to take us into Kingston for a movie. None of us have been further than the village store, so naturally we all were eager to go. Since Susie's father had driven up to see her last weekend, we had two cars and plenty of room for eleven people. All of us dressed up. I finally got to wear my new flowered skirt, and when I washed my face and combed my hair, I noticed that aside from a small border of pimples down my hairline, my skin shone clear and rosy tan. I looked good. All of us looked good—clean, shiny and unfamiliar in our dress-up clothes. The town seemed packed with people, and I felt like a hick come down from the hills—which I was.

The movie, *Yankee Doodle Dandy*, was fun, and afterwards, we stopped at an ice-cream place for cones. Andrea, Roger and I were standing outside waiting for the others. We were licking one another's cones—I had vanilla, Andrea strawberry, and Roger coconut, when two teenage boys came by and stopped in front of us. They looked like some of the local boys we see sometimes down by the swimming hole. They were smiling at us, so we smiled back. Then one of them said, "Nigger!"

Roger didn't hear, and he leaned forward, smiling, and said, "Pardon?" With strangers, his manners tend to be excellent.

"Nigger lover!" said the boy, advancing on Roger.

Roger looked at me, confused, but before I

could say anything, Andrea stepped forward and said, in her best schoolmarm voice, "You shouldn't use words unless you know how to spell them." Her face was composed, and she peered at the boy as if he was six years old.

His head snapped back, surprised, and I began laughing. Behind me I heard Jerry laugh, and knew he had come out of the store too. Roger wasn't laughing though. Suddenly he stiffened, clenched his fists, and looked as if he was going to charge. But Jerry moved down, in front of Andrea, and put an arm on Roger's shoulder.

"What's going on?" Mrs. Horne stood behind us, an ice-cream cone in her hand. Susie, Dorothy and Bobby stood around her, licking their cones and watching the two strange boys as if they were specimens in our nature museum. Susie's father also came through the door and repeated, "What's going on?"

"Would you care to repeat what you just said?" Jerry asked the boy. "Or would you rather spell it?"

They slunk off, and Susie's father said, "Now what was that all about?"

I knew it was going to happen—knew it because I had moved close to her and was there when her calm, haughty schoolmarm face turned into the frightened, hurt face of an eleven-year-old girl. Andrea cried—for the first time that summer, she cried. I held her against me, and she cried.

Everybody wanted to sit next to her at dinner that night, and she had to tell over and over again how she had humiliated the two bigots.

"Just one more time," somebody or other begged, and when she finished telling it, then I had to or Roger or Jerry.

"I miss all the fun," Jason complained. He had been the last to come out.

We all laughed each time we heard it, and then I said, not wanting the laughter to fade, not wanting to think about Andrea's wet face, "Let's have a spelling bee tonight."

"After punchball," said Roger.

"Naturally," I told him, "but we don't have to play so long."

I had Andrea, Fred and Bobby on my team, and Jerry had Roger, Susie, Jason and Dorothy on his. Mrs. Horne flipped through *Hiawatha* for the words. When I tripped up on *Minnehaha*, Jerry laughed, but I had the last laugh when he got hopelessly wrapped up in *Gitche Gumee*. Andrea spelled everything right from *whippoorwill* to *lamentation*. Roger struggled through *heron* but buckled under *melancholy*. Dorothy was allowed to consult with Jerry; and Fred, Bobby, Susie and Jason ran neck and neck for last place.

Of course my team won. With Andrea on my side, we couldn't lose. We held ten rounds, and the winning team made lemonade for the losers.

The spelling bee was only the first in a series of festivities. Every night this week we have had a special event. By Wednesday we weren't even playing our evening punchball game. Monday night we had a mock marriage. Roger was the bride, Dorothy the groom, Jason the maid of honor, and Bobby and Fred the bridesmaids. Susie was best man, and Andrea the minister. Mrs. Horne was flower girl, and Jerry and I were the bride's parents in reverse. He was the mother and I the father.

We dressed Roger in some old sheets and made a flower wreath for his hair. I smeared Mrs. Horne's lipstick over his mouth and cheeks. He made a wonderfully funny bride, talking in a girl's high voice (actually not much higher than his own), and crying noisily throughout the ceremony.

Dorothy wore a pair of Jason's overalls, and we tucked her hair underneath a straw sun hat of Mrs. Horne's.

We even had a proper wedding cake when the ceremony ended, made of bought coconut cupcakes tiered up on toothpicks.

Tuesday night we held a masquerade ball, and all day long we worked on costumes. Jerry came as a Christmas tree. He covered himself with branches studded with silver paper balls, gum wrappers, jacks, pieces of puzzles—anything and everything. He looked great but couldn't sit down. I came as a bathroom. I draped myself in towels and hung toothbrushes, toothpaste, soap, washcloths, combs, and brushes all over me. On my head was a crown made out of two toilet-paper rolls. Dorothy, naturally, came as Lady Godiva (in a bathing suit), and Fred was her horse. Andrea and Susie came as Siamese twins, wearing each other's clothes sewn together at the side. Roger was a ghost, Bobby a pirate, and Jason, Tarzan.

Wednesday we had an amateur hour. Everybody had to perform. Dorothy brought her worms and recited a poem that Jerry had taught her.

> Ooey Gooey was a worm
> A mighty worm was he;
> He sat upon a railroad track
> The train he did not see. . . .
> Oooey Gooey!

But Bobby won first prize, unanimously, by standing on his head for five minutes and whistling "East Side, West Side."

Thursday was a scavenger hunt, and tonight we're having a hootenanny grab-bag party. Everybody is supposed to bring a gift—either something you own or something you can buy for less than ten cents at the general store. I took some of the kids down this morning but we were all honor bound not to peek at what each other bought.

Jerry and I are working on a big, bang-up initiation night next week. Everybody up here will have to pass an initiation rite, and then he/she will become a life member in the Secret Society of Supersummerstars. They will receive special membership cards with their names framed in silver stars.

"You'll have to go through an initiation too," Roger said this morning. "Fred, Andrea and I will work up something for the two of you. Don't think you're going to get off easy."

Tomorrow Dr. Horne will be coming up. Mrs. Horne is planning to make a leg of lamb, and today she baked a big batch of oatmeal-raisin cookies, his favorite. A couple of times this week she said, "I can't wait to tell Eddie."

When he comes, this charmed week will end. I guess it will begin again after he goes. But I wish we could shut out the world—bar the doors, put up Keep Out signs everywhere. I wish we could always stay the way we are—never change, never go back to the city and stop seeing each other. I want to be a part of everybody's life here, and I want them to be a part of my life—forever.

Today Dorothy let me brush her hair again. She still stood stiffly in front of me, and I kept thinking, if I pull her over to me, maybe she'll nestle against my arm the way she does with Jerry. I thought about trying but I'm still afraid she'll turn away. But next time, for sure, I'll try.

Chapter 12

August 16, 1943: I hope there will be a next time.

Dorothy is in the hospital, very sick. Mrs. Horne is with her, and Jerry and I are alone here with the kids. She called tonight and said Dorothy was still unconscious. She said they thought now that it was a diabetic coma, and that they are going to give her insulin. She sounded hopeful. One of the doctors said they'd had another case like this with an eight-year-old girl and that the insulin brought her out of the coma. Mrs. Horne has been trying to contact Dorothy's mother, but so far no luck.

Susie is asleep in my bunk tonight. She was afraid to sleep upstairs, afraid to sleep on her own bed because that's where Dorothy lay before the ambulance came for her. Susie cried, and even though Andrea offered to sleep in Susie's bed tonight, it didn't help. So I brought her down here with me, and she's asleep now.

Jerry is staying upstairs with the boys. They seem okay, so far. We had fresh corn for dinner. It was the first batch of the season, and Mrs. Horne had just come back from the greengrocer with it when Dorothy became sick.

Jerry and I were in the barn, making preparations for tonight's initiation. None of the kids were supposed to look in. It was all going to be one huge surprise. But they lingered outside, giggling and threatening to peek.

"Get away, Roger," Jerry yelled. "Why don't you take all the kids up to the field and play punchball?"

"We'd rather stay here," from Andrea. "And remember, you'd better go easy on us, because tomorrow the worm turns, and *you're* going to be initiated."

I giggled when she said "worm turns," because in the final phase of the initiation, each blindfolded initiate would have to put his/her hand into Dorothy's can of worms.

"Little does she know," whispered Jerry. He was working on a rope cage that would swing from one of the rafters. Each of the kids would be suspended in the cage, and pushed back and forth, while one of us kept yelling, "Watch out, the rope's breaking."

We had other torments to work out, including: The Cavern of Spiders, which consisted of long strings of wet thread to dangle in their faces; The Quicksand Quagmire—a muddy spot behind the barn for them to walk through barefoot; and The Cup of Hemlock—sweetened ketchup for them to drink.

Each kid would be taken, blindfolded and bare-foot, from the house by the two of us, masked and sheeted. The others would have to wait on the back porch for their turns. We hoped they would hear the shrieks and cries from each of their predecessors.

"I think the two of us shouldn't speak at all until the initiation is over," Jerry said.

"What do we do when they ask questions?"

"Just moan and groan."

"But we have to tell them they are going into The Quicksand Quagmire or that we're dangling them over The Perilous Precipice."

"All right. Maybe I can just tell them that in a deep, solemn voice."

"Okay, but remember, I have to yell, 'Watch out, the rope's breaking.' I can disguise my voice and try to sound like Dorothy."

"Okay. But then, when it's over, and we take off their blindfolds, we can both say together, 'Congratulations, Brother' or 'Sister. You've successfully walked through the Desert of Despair, dangled over The Perilous Precipice, risen out of The Quicksand Quagmire. . . .' "

"Jerry!" Dorothy was standing inside the barn, her thumb in her mouth.

"Hey, Dorothy," Jerry said, "you can't be in here. It's all got to be a big surprise tonight."

"I don't want a big surprise tonight."

"Andrea," I yelled, "why don't you take Dorothy up to the house and do a puzzle with her or something?"

"Come on out, Dorothy, we'll do a puzzle," Andrea yelled.

"I don't want to do a puzzle."

"We'll dress up your doll. Come on out. I can't come in."

"I don't want to play with my doll. Jerry! Jerry! I want to go home. I want my mother."

"Look, Dorothy, I'll be finished in a little while, and then I'll tell you a story. All right?"

"My head hurts me."

"Why don't you go lie down for a while?" I suggested.

Suddenly we heard the car coming up the road.

"There's Mrs. Horne," I said. "Why don't you go see what she brought back from the market?"

"Go ahead, Dorothy," Jerry said. "I'll be finished soon."

Dorothy ran out and we could hear her crying, "Frances, Frances, my head hurts."

I was hobbling around because yesterday, down at the stream, I sprained my ankle, tripping over a rock. It was still swollen but Mrs. Horne had tied a tight bandage around my foot so that I could move around. It hurt but I was determined not to delay the initiation. This promised to be another

week like the last. Tonight the kids would be initiated, tomorrow Jerry and myself. Wednesday we
were to have our first secret ceremony around an
outside campfire, with shadows, incantations,
chantings and maybe a few riddles and marshmallows. Thursday— We hadn't gotten up to
Thursday yet.

"Can you come up the ladder and help me loop
this rope over the rafter? I need you to hold an
end, but don't do it if it hurts too much."

It hurt, but painfully, slowly, I hoisted myself
up, trying to put most of the weight on my other
leg. And I was nearly all the way up the ladder
when I heard her scream.

"Gloria!"

It was Mrs. Horne screaming. People don't
scream the way she was screaming.

I came down the ladder ten times as quickly as
I'd gone up and flew off to the house, forgetting
all about my swollen ankle. I could hear Mrs.
Horne still screaming my name, and all I could
think was that something or someone was trying
to kill her.

They were in the girls' bedroom. Dorothy lay
on Susie's bed, and Mrs. Horne was bending over
her. Dorothy's eyes were rolling up in their sockets
and her mouth foamed.

"My God, I don't know what's wrong with her.
My God!"

"Dorothy," I yelled, as if she was a long way off,
"Dorothy, what's wrong?"

"She said her head hurt her, and I told her to lie down. I brought her in here to put her down but she passed out right at the door."

"Dorothy! Dorothy!" I shouted.

"Oh my God! What should I do?" She was sobbing now, and I yelled at her, "Call the doctor. Hurry up! Call the doctor."

"Oh yes, I'll do that—but Dorothy?"

"Hurry! I'll stay with her. Hurry!"

I tried to pick Dorothy up but she lay like a dead weight on the bed. I propped a pillow under her head and tried to support her with my arm around her shoulders. Her head lolled back and forth, and she breathed in great, noisy gasps.

"What is it? What's happening?" The voice was Jerry's, but I couldn't take the time to look at him.

"Oh no! What's wrong with her? Oh, NO!"

"Get out of here, Jerry," I yelled, "and keep the kids away. Wait—bring me a wet cloth. Hurry!"

I could hear him crying as he brought me the cloth, and I said more gently, "Go away now, Jerry. She'll be okay."

I dabbed at her face; a network of red and blue veins spread over her cheeks. I wiped away the foam from her mouth and whispered, "Dorothy? Dorothy? Are you all right? Can you hear me?"

I could feel her body stiffening in my arms, and I tried to bring her closer to me, to shelter her. From what? Her breathing continued deep and noisy.

"He's coming. He's on his way. I don't think he

believed me but he'll be here in fifteen minutes. I brought this bottle of smelling salts. Maybe we should try it."

I held the vile-smelling bottle under Dorothy's nose, and her head flung itself back.

"See, see!" I cried. "That's a good sign."

Mrs. Horne's voice was high and shaky. "What could have happened to her? It just came on so suddenly. Could it be epilepsy? Maybe that's what it is. Or maybe she fell and hit her head. She said she had a headache. Oh my God, what's wrong with her?"

I held her until the doctor arrived. I wet her face and listened to her deep, heavy gasps. Later, when the ambulance arrived, they put her in an oxygen tent. When I looked through the back window of the ambulance before they drove off for the hospital, I could see her lying there with her yellow ribbons untied at the ends of her braids.

"Mrs. Horne thinks she's going to be all right," I told everybody after she called from the hospital. "They're giving her insulin, and they think it will bring her out of the coma."

August 17, 1943: Dorothy died at 4:30 this morning. The phone woke me at 5. I could hear it a long way off in my sleep, and it took at least ten rings before I reached it. Jerry was coming down the stairs as I picked it up. The rest of the kids slept on.

"Did I wake you?" Mrs. Horne's voice was soft and gentle.

"That's all right. How is she?"

"She's dead. She died a little while ago. I shouldn't have phoned you but I'm all alone here. Eddie is on his way up. He's been trying to find Lila all night. She doesn't know her child is dead. She only has the one, and she doesn't know she's dead."

"What is it?" Jerry was whispering. "How's Dorothy?"

I shook my head, and he sat down on the floor.

"Where are you now, Mrs. Horne?"

"I'm at the hospital waiting for Eddie. I spoke to him at 2 before they even knew she was dying. At 2 the doctor even thought she was responding, but Eddie said he was going to come up anyway. He was going over to Lila's house one more time and if she wasn't there, he'd leave another note for her, but then he was coming up. I'm waiting for him now."

"What do you want us to do?"

"Nothing. Don't say anything to the kids. Eddie and I will tell them. Just act like it's a normal day. We should be back by dinner. Can you manage?"

"Sure we can. Don't worry about us. We'll be fine."

"They wouldn't even let me stay with her at the end. They made me go out of the room while they were working on her. She was all alone at the end.

She didn't even have her mother with her, and they made me go outside."

"She wasn't even conscious, Mrs. Horne. She didn't know."

She was crying now, so I said, "You did everything you could for her. Even if her mother had been there, she couldn't have done any more."

"Why wouldn't they let me stay? She was such a little girl."

"Mrs. Horne, can you get a cup of coffee there? Maybe you should go and get a cup of coffee."

"I will, Gloria. Thanks, Gloria. I'll be all right but I had to talk to somebody because I'm all alone here and Eddie won't be up for another couple of hours."

"We can go on talking."

"No, no, I'm all right now. I feel better now. I'm going to get some coffee now. Thanks, Gloria."

Jerry was sitting on the floor. He wasn't crying but his face was pale and quivering. "What did she die of? What was it?"

"I forgot to ask. But let's go outside. Otherwise we'll wake up the kids. She doesn't want us to tell them. Dr. Horne is coming up to meet her at the hospital but he still hasn't been able to reach Dorothy's mother."

Jerry nodded and stood up. The two of us moved outside onto the porch. It was already day, and the birds were noisy in the morning's quiet. Nothing had changed since yesterday except that Dorothy was dead.

"She said her head hurt her," Jerry said. "I didn't really believe her."

"Never mind," I told him. "It wouldn't have made any difference."

"Maybe it would," he cried. "Maybe if I had listened to her . . . maybe if I had tried to help . . ."

"It wouldn't have mattered."

"I couldn't do anything for her. When I saw her lying there all discolored and unconscious, it made me sick to my stomach. I had to go outside and put my head down. I thought I was going to faint. I couldn't do anything for her. I couldn't help her. She asked me to help her but I couldn't."

"You did help her, Jerry," I told him. "When she was alive you made her happy. You heard what her mother said. You did a lot for her."

"But I couldn't help her when she was dying. You could. You were the only one who did."

He was crying and I cried too. I cried for him because he was my friend and he was suffering. But I cried for Dorothy and I cried for myself too. Even though I had held her in my arms while she was dying, I had never done anything for her when she was alive. And now it was too late.

Chapter 13

Our summer issue of *Wings* (June '44) has a poem of Jerry's in it called "Night Sky." Someone told me he wrote it because a friend of his brother's died fighting on one of the Pacific islands. It really hit me.

> If I could know for sure
> That the sky is a giant graveyard
> I might not grieve.
> If I could know
> That each star is planted there
> For someone who died young
> I might not mourn
> So much.

I have seen young boys
Who left their stickball games,
Their unhinged stamps in albums,
To go and die on some Pacific island
Where the sun shines on a snow-white beach.
I have read of babies
Killed in bombings
Before their lips could shape a smile.

And I have known a young girl
with long, shiny braids
Who died one summer
With yellow ribbons in her hair.

I want to watch the night sky
And remember them.
I want to say—There, that one is Laura—
She had the bluest eyes.
And see, that bright, shiny one's for Hal—
He never cried.

It is enough their dreams were never finished.
Why should they be forgotten too?
Life must offer some sweets
To those of us who live on
And remember.
Life must mark the ones who die young,
Must flash their youth and beauty
Across an endless sky
And let their short lives burn through
Infinite galaxies of remembered stars.

It reminded me of last summer. Jerry's poems this past year have all reminded me of last summer. They deal with children and laughter and big skies with bright stars. And many of them deal with death.

I haven't written anything about last summer except what's in my diary. All my stories this year have been fairy tales, fantasies—bigger and better icicles and leaves. One day I'll take last summer out and maybe I'll be able to write about it. But for now I want to keep it tucked inside me. I don't want to let it out.

When Jerry came in to gather his things up this afternoon, I hung around waiting for a chance to talk to him. We haven't spoken much in the last couple of months but I wanted to talk to him once more before the vacation. Not only about his poem, but that would give me a chance to begin.

"I liked your poem, Jerry," I told him, clearing my throat and looking half at him and half over his head.

"Oh?" He wasn't expecting me to talk, and he turned, startled, to look at me. "Thanks." Of course, he was blushing again.

"It's a very good poem."

"Thanks."

Now I had to say something else. Now I had to thank him, but before I could, he said, "Do you ever think about Dorothy?"

"Well sure I do. Sure. Sometimes."

"Me too," he said, ". . . sometimes. Not the way

I did at first. Everything seems to fade, doesn't it?"

"Not everything. I still remember that night we watched for shooting stars. Your poem reminds me of that night. That's another reason I like it so much."

Now we were looking at each other, almost smiling. Jerry has grown this past year. He must be nearly six feet tall, and still chunky. Could I still throw him? I wondered. Could I catch him off guard, get him in a headlock, weaken his stance? Better than . . . better than . . . better than!

It was still there, to my shame—my need to contend against him. I should have disguised it, should have remembered the summer, should not have allowed our friendship to fade.

But it wasn't only me. Maybe I explode and yell, and maybe Jerry doesn't. But he hangs on. He never gives in. All our little disputes and differences could have been negotiated but he doesn't negotiate—ever. We could have talked things over. We could have compromised. I wasn't the only one. He could have tried too.

The final straw came when he accepted Maude Green's story, "Senior Prom."

"You had no right," I told him. "You know how I feel about her and her sappy stories."

"No, I don't," he said weakly. (A trick. He always pretends ignorance of my feelings but he knows. He always knows how I feel.)

"Yes, you do," I exploded. "I told you a million times I don't want that kind of trash in *Wings*. We're supposed to be a literary magazine, remember, not *True Confessions*."

"Frank said it was okay, and Mrs. Horne liked it."

"You went over my head. You always go over my head. You did with the deadlines in the last issue. You let Elsie Brier get her poems in five days late, and you okayed the artwork for the centerfold before I even saw it, and you . . ."

"Gloria, we're supposed to share the work. We can't both do everything."

"I can't trust *you* to do anything. Maude Green is a birdbrain."

"The kids like her stories, and just because she has a light touch doesn't mean she's a birdbrain. People enjoy humor. Oscar Wilde was no mental giant but people enjoyed his wit and humor."

"Why are you bringing up Oscar Wilde all of a sudden?"

"I don't know. Why shouldn't I?"

"Because you mean something else. You always bring him up."

"I don't know what you're talking about, Gloria, but forget about Oscar Wilde."

"I don't want to forget about Oscar Wilde. You're just trying to insult me, but I'm not going to stand for it."

That was our last fight. Now the year was over,

and for the past few months we had barely spoken to each other.

A few weeks ago, Mrs. Horne asked me to stay after everybody else had gone.

"Jerry is quitting," she told me.

"What?"

"He doesn't want to be on the staff next year. He *says* he's too involved with other school activities." She was looking at me seriously—accusingly, I thought.

"Well, it's not my fault."

"I never said it was."

"No, but you think it is."

She remained silent.

"You always think it's my fault. You always take his part. Every little argument, I know you think I'm wrong. But he's stubborn. You don't know how stubborn he is. Even though everybody thinks he's such a weak sister, he's like a mule when he makes up his mind."

"I never thought he was a weak sister."

"Nobody can say I pick fights with him. I've been getting along with everybody this year."

"Well . . ."

". . . nearly everybody. But he purposely does things to irritate me. He took Maude Green's story. . . ."

"It's a good story. The kids enjoy her stuff."

". . . and he didn't really edit that long interview with Paul Robeson, and he . . ."

"Gloria! He's quitting, Gloria. Stop attacking him. You're going to be editor-in-chief all by yourself, and may heaven protect the rest of us!"

She was smiling, so I smiled too, and I sat on the edge of her desk, and we talked about next year when I would be editor-in-chief all by myself. I gloated as she continued to talk. It was all mine now, the editorship of *Wings*, all mine! She began talking about Roger and Jason and Dr. Horne. She talked about this summer. The boys were going to camp, and she and her husband were taking a trip to Mexico. They weren't going to be spending any time at all at their country place. All mine! Only mine!

"And what will you be doing, Gloria?"

I came down to earth. Thump! "Uh . . . I'm going to get a job. My mother thinks I should make some money."

"What kind of a job?"

"I'm not sure. One of my uncles has a cleaning store, and I might be able to work there."

"The boys keep asking for you," she said softly. "They tell all their friends that nobody can hit the ball as far as you in punchball."

"I think about them too."

"I saw Lila last week."

"Oh? How is she?"

"Back to work full time now. She's a little thinner, a little more nervous. It doesn't show but it's there all right. Poor thing, I'll never forget how she cried. . . . There wasn't anything she could have done. How could anyone know there was such a huge brain tumor in such a little child?"

"Nobody could have done anything."

"No, I guess not. What a terrible time it was!"

"No," I cried fiercely, "it was a wonderful time. Not Dorothy dying—that was terrible. That shouldn't have happened. But the rest of it—as long as it lasted—it was all summer—except for Dorothy."

Maybe for Mrs. Horne it was only one of many summers, but for me it was The Summer. Maybe one day, like her, I would have many summers in my life that counted. Maybe one day I would spend them again with people whom I cared for, and who cared for me. The beginnings were there, inside me, waiting. I knew, one day, it was going to happen. But for now, I had my editorship. I wanted it now, more than anything else.

Mrs. Horne nodded vaguely. "We should have a reunion one of these days," she said, and I agreed. I knew we never would. She always said we should, but I knew we wouldn't. I knew it was over.

My friendship with Jerry was over too, and now he had given me a farewell present. Just as Mondamin had given Hiawatha the gift of corn, Jerry was giving me the editorship of *Wings*.

Why? He could have hung on another year and shared it with me. Why was he giving it to me all of a sudden?

Was it pity?

Long he looked at Hiawatha,
Looked with pity and compassion

He pitied me. I know that now. Last summer
when I asked him over and over again why he
never grew angry at me when I was so bitchy, he
never answered. He kept saying, "Never mind."
Maybe I thought then there might be another
reason. Now I know it was pity. Just the same
way he never got angry at Dorothy when she was
bratty and difficult. He pitied Dorothy, and he
pitied me.

I don't want his pity, but a gift's a gift. And I
need the editorship more right now than I need
anything else in the world. So I'll take it, whatever
his reasons. But I wanted to thank him this afternoon. I can't take anything from him, from anybody, for nothing.

We stood there looking at each other, nearly
smiling, and I thought, now I can thank him. Now
I can pay him back. But Elsie Brier came in the
door, hollering, "Come on, Jerry, they're all waiting for us."

She's been hanging on him all year, but he
doesn't seem to mind. He just turned even redder
than before, mumbled something about having to
go, and hurried out of the room.

Maybe if she hadn't come he would have told
me why he quit. Maybe it didn't have anything to
do with me. He's so busy now—treasurer of the

student council, president of the Victory Corps, captain of the debating team, and undisputed poet laureate of the school. He's busy with his friends too, so maybe he simply doesn't have the time. Probably it didn't have anything to do with me at all—and if it did, it's not my fault. Nothing would have made *me* give it up.

But I should have thanked him anyway, and that hurt. I don't want to take anything from him for nothing. I sat down at my desk after he left, and suffered. Last summer was far away now. Would it fade for good one day? Was there no way I could find my way back to it? I felt like yelling. I felt like kicking something. Maude Green came into the room, but when she saw me there, she turned right around and started out again.

"Maude!" I shouted.

"What?" she said nervously.

"Your story— 'Senior Prom'—I think— I mean—a lot of kids told me they like it."

"Thanks, Gloria," she said. "Thanks a lot."

But it had nothing to do with her. I was only paying Jerry back.